USA TODAY BESTSELLING AUTHOR
CLAIRE SHAW

ROAD WRECKERS

CHAOS

ROAD WRECKERS MC

CHAOS

ROAD WRECKERS MC
BOOK ONE

By
Claire Shaw

CHAOS

COPYRIGHT

Claire Shaw 2022
All Rights Reserved

The characters, places, and names are fiction and have been created by the author.
Any similarities to real life are coincidental.

This book may not be resold or given to others.
This book or portions of the book may not be reproduced in any form without written consent from the author.

CLAIRE SHAW

CONTENTS

COPYRIGHT	III
CONTENTS	V
DISCLAIMER	VII
BLURB	IX
ONE	1
Chaos	1
TWO	7
Olivia	7
THREE	12
Chaos	12
FOUR	18
Olivia	18
FIVE	26
Chaos	26
SIX	34
Olivia	34
SEVEN	41
Chaos	41
EIGHT	49
Olivia	49
NINE	58
Chaos	58
TEN	68
Olivia	68
ELEVEN	76
Chaos	76
TWELVE	82
Olivia	82
THIRTEEN	89
Chaos	89
FOURTEEN	101
Olivia	101
FIFTEEN	107
Chaos	107
SIXTEEN	112
Olivia	112
SEVENTEEN	118
Chaos	118
EIGHTEEN	125
Olivia	125
NINETEEN	132
Chaos	132
TWENTY	141

Olivia	141
DEDICATION	145
SERIES ORDER	147
OTHER BOOKS BY CLAIRE	149
ABOUT THE AUTHOR	151
SOCIAL LINKS	153

CHAOS

DISCLAIMER

This book is for 18+ only.
Contains adult themes, sexual violence, and adult language.

Cover designs – Coffin Print Designs.

Editor & Formatting – Maria Lazarou – Obsessed By Books Designs.

BLURB

OLIVIA

This MC princess is not living a fairy-tale.
How do you trust a man you don't know, with your life?
I've trusted the men in my life before and look where that's got me. In a right bloody mess!
Men only think with one brain and it's not the one in their heads.
Can Chaos and his brothers restore not only my faith in men but also bikers?
Will this Cinderella get her happy ever after, or remain in a nightmare?

CHAOS

What should have been a normal business deal is now so much more complicated.

This is not how my brothers and I do business, but how could I say no when she's part of the deal?
All I have to do is keep her safe, that's it.

Except, she's under my skin & melting the cold, black ice in my heart.
I need to be on my game to protect her, does that mean I need to stay hands-off?

Time will tell if she's my queen or my biggest mistake.

Claire Shaw

ONE

CHAOS

"CHURCH" I bellow as I storm through the main room, heading for our sanctuary.

I don't look behind me, I can hear the chairs scraping along the floor as they all get up to follow me. I head into the sanctuary and take my seat at the head of the table and my brothers slowly file in and take their seats.

Mayhem, my VP is on my right with Riot taking the Sergeant At Arms seat on my left. Psycho, true to his name, takes the Enforcer's seat next to Riot. Dolla our money man, Treasurer is next to Mayhem, then Tracker, our Road Captain and finally bringing up the rear is our tech hacker genius Keys.

Our Officer's table is complete.

I slide the wooden gavel into my right hand, feeling the weight of responsibility for this bunch of misfits settle on my shoulders. Lifting it and I bring it down with a heavy hand. We have a lot to get through today, and they tend to go off on a tangent when left too far off the leash.

Just before speaking, I feel a heavy lump on each side of my legs. Looking down I notice my two Rottweilers, King and Raze scoot in with the guys. Rubbing each of their heads, I start Church.

"Dolla, how are we banking?"

He opens his ledger and shuffles some papers.

"Looking healthy. Garage is well into the black and getting busier. Might need to look at adding another mechanic we trust or a prospect. Wreckers are also into the black and lining our pockets nicely. New food and cocktail menus have increased profits. The new manager is working a treat. He's got a lot of good ideas. Might be worth looking at opening another location. Twisted Skin percentage is looking good. Prospect is running the business well."

I tune the rest of it out as Dolla goes over the figures of each business and the profits, plus how he is laundering the money from our side and not exactly legal business through each of the legal businesses. He thinks maybe adding another business or location would be a good idea but I don't want to spread us too thin.

"Thanks, Dolla. I'll think about opening a second location. If you can get me costs and also possible locations, projections, etc. The usual and I'll consider it."

Dolla nods at me and makes a note on his papers.

"Are we all on plan for the next run?" I ask looking at Psycho.

"Yeah," he growls at me

Man of little words is our Psycho but his attention to

detail is impeccable, which is why he organises our runs. Our less than legal side of the business is bringing drugs in through the docks and getting them to where they need to go. Don't dabble ourselves in the distribution, we're more the middle shipping man.

"Good, we've got no time for fuck ups," I warn.

Psycho just hits me with a look that says, *who the fuck ya telling?* I stare back with a, *just be on it,* look. Mayhem joins in with a, *we got this,* look. *A fuck you* are sent back to both of them.

Pair of arseholes always trying my patience.

"Use your words fuckers," Riot moans.

"Jealous?" Mayhem snarks back.

In typical Psycho fashion, he rolls his eyes and flicks Riot the finger.

"Set of clever fuckers," he grumbles, making us all chuckle

We've been best friends since we were kids, we know each other better than brothers. It sometimes pisses the others off when we speak through looks, but we know what the others are saying. The three of us could have a full conversation without words.

"Right now, to the fun stuff. Tracker we all set for Into The Wind rally?"

The rally is a yearly bike rally in Yorkshire, always a good weekend. Meeting up with support clubs, conduct a little business, and have a little fun. The boys need to relax and let off a little steam.

"Yeah, routes planned, I've checked everyone's bikes

already but I'll double-check day or so before too. Camping equipment has been checked and made sure everything is packed ready to load in the van with the prospect to follow us."

Tracker is our Road Captain and it's his job to plan our routes, make sure all our bikes are in shape and plan for any issues.

"Good, Riot, I've arranged with Judge of Tribal Bones to meet up. They are due their last payment. Need you and Mayhem with me. Psycho, I want you close but not too close. Something feels off to me, so need you on watch, all of you."

Tribal Bones is an MC we are friendly with through our loan-sharking business. Another not-so-legal way of earning for the club. Judge, who is the Tribal Prez, was friends with my dad. They go way back to being a couple of punks on bikes in the sixties. Recently, he got a new VP, Dyno since his son Voodoo went missing. I don't trust that fucking twat Dyno as far as I could throw him. Jacked-up wannabe is what he is and definitely not a man of his word.

"Yeah, that new VP is a snake if I ever meet one," Mayhem grumbles.

"Even I wouldn't touch him," Riot joins in, and we all look at him with raised eyebrows.

"Fuck off the lot of you. He's a cockwomble if ever I saw one and I do have fucking standards."

Yeah, Riot can be a bit of a manwhore when he wants to be and I mean a manwhore. He's gay and proud. Makes no difference to me or the club where he wants to stick his dick. Each to their own and whatever or whoever makes him happy is all we care about.

"Think we need to look into them a little closer. Never sat right with me the way Voodoo just disappeared," Mayhem says while rubbing his chin.

"I agree. Keys do your magic and see what you can dig up on the fucker."

Keys nods his understanding. These fuckers need to be more talkative at times.

"Lastly, I want to bring Twisted to the table. He's currently our longest serving Prospect. He's proved himself numerous times and the tattoo shop he talked us into backing has more than shown he's got a good eye for business and that he's committed to the future of the club. I say we see how he is at the rally and then look into patching him."

I leave that there for a minute for them all to think it over.

"Bring him to meet with Tribal Bones and see how he does. A little test if he can hold his tongue," Mayhem suggests.

This is why he's, my VP. He's good at bouncing ideas off but also at keeping me sane.

"You got Logan sorted for the rally?" I ask.

Mayhem is a single parent to a four-year-old little mischief called Logan. As his uncles, we love the little tyke and spoil him when he's around the club. He's the next generation and a mini biker in the making. Much to Babs annoyance his first word was *'fuck.'* Babs is Mayhem's mum. She and his dad Leon help Mayhem raise Logan. Logan had a rough start thanks to his bitch of a mum, but the kids thriving now.

"Yeah, he is staying the rents for the weekend, he can't wait."

Mayhem smirks knowing full well Logan is going to be spoilt all weekend. Kid loves his granny and pops. The whole club loves Babs and Leon; they are family and come to all our BBQs' and gatherings. Supporting Mayhem's decision to be a part of the club and taking us all on as their own. Babs treats all us brothers like we're her sons too. Checking were okay, looking after us when we get sick, and lecturing us when needed. The woman might be small but I wouldn't piss her off.

TWO

OLIVIA

I'M on my hands and knees in the communal bathroom, scrubbing around the toilets. Why can't men learn to hit the bowl and not the floor? I mean seriously, how hard can it be to aim that thing between their legs. You surely just point it in the direction you want to aim, but no, they just stand there and pee where they bloody well like, completely missing. Sounds about right for the twat waffles around here. I remember a time when I loved being at the clubhouse with my dad and his brothers. It's all changed now and not in a good way.

"Liv where the fuck are you girl?" Bellows Guts.

Jesus, he's the worst of them. He likes to tell people he's called Guts because he guts people who cross him. Yeah, I'd like to see him try. It's because he has the biggest gut or beer belly in the club. Man's a lazy pig.

"In here Guts."

The door to the bathroom slams open.

"Need you to clean my room. It's a bit of a mess," he growls at me.

I hold in the urge to roll my eyes. A bit of a mess, what he means is that he's got so drunk again that he doesn't know what he's been doing. That tends to lead him to being sick all over and sometimes not making it to the bathroom in time.

Perfect.

Guts is an alcoholic which is now causing issues with his liver and kidneys.

"I'll finish here and get straight on it Guts."

"No. Do it now, I'm heading into Church and I want it done by the time we're finished," he growls at me with a menacing snarl.

"Okay Guts."

I move away from the toilet and try to move past him.

"You're getting awful pretty Liv. Really coming into your own," he says as he trails a dirty fat finger down my cheek, neck, and across the top of my chest.

Praying he doesn't go any further and leaves me alone, I stay still and try not to meet his eyes.

"Guts, Church now," comes from the hallway.

"Saved at the last minute this time girl, but don't worry, I'll be having a taste soon."

With his parting threat, he moves away and heads down the hallway to the main room and Church. I finally release the breath I didn't realise I was holding.

Filthy fucker.

I grab the cleaning supplies, the clean bedding I need,

and head to Guts' room. The smell of piss and sick hits me as I open the door. I wrap the bandana around the lower half of my face, to help with the smell. The bandana has lavender oil on it to help mask the smells as much as possible. Stripping the bed and cleaning the mess takes about thirty minutes. I open a window to let the smell out and fresh air in. Dumping the dirty soiled bedding in the laundry room, I put it on a boil wash.

That man needs putting down.

I have a list of jobs that need doing today and I could really do without this shit. I make it back into the main room and start to straighten up the tables, collecting the empties. They should be out of Church soon and will all want serving at the bar. Getting everything ready for them, I can suddenly hear shouting from Church. My ears prick up when I hear my name.

As if moving on their own, my feet take me closer to the closed doors so I can hear a little better. The voices are muffled through the door and I'm struggling to hear. I catch my name again and then the scrape of chairs moving on the floor making me jump. I move quickly back behind the bar so it doesn't look like I was listening. The brothers file out, some looking pissed off and others with creepy smirks on their faces. I keep busy behind the bar, wiping down shelves and getting drinks.

"Liv, get me a beer," demands Lizard as he slides up to the bar

Nodding, I quickly get him a one.

"Fuck you're so slow, useless bitch," he sneers as he walks away.

Lizard is one of Dyno and Guts' cronies. Them joined with Rattle are the ones who have come in and ruined my dad's club. They are gross and nasty, treat others like they are beneath them. They are the dregs of the club, not good brothers at all.

"Olivia sweetheart, you got a minute?" My dad asks.

"Of course, dad, what's up?" I ask, finding him stood at the end of the bar.

"Join me in my office," he says before walking away.

It must be serious as usually; he would just tell me here. Worried even more now, I follow him down the corridor to his office. I can see the Wanker crew as I like to call them grinning at me.

Yeah, this isn't going to be good if they are happy about it.

"Sit down honey," Dad says as I join him in his office, closing the door behind me.

I slowly sink into the chair in front of his desk and silently I wait for him to speak.

"Sweetheart, I know I haven't been the dad you deserve. You are very special and even though I don't show it often, I love you very much."

Great way to start, now I'm really nervous.

He's right, he's not always been the best dad. My mum died when I was born, so he was suddenly a single parent to a baby and my brother, who was just a toddler. He did his best but while running the club and trying to raise us, it didn't leave a lot of time for love. He's not a bad dad, never neglectful but just not present. He struggles to show his love, but I know he loves me.

"I really do love you and your brother, wherever he is," he continues.

My brother has been missing for a few weeks now. Dad is trying to find him, it's unlike Voodoo to go missing like this and not be in touch. He always stays in touch.

"Dad, I love you too. You might not tell me you love me often I feel your love. Voodoo will be okay and back soon. Don't give up hope," I beg him.

"Oh sweetheart, everything I do is to keep you safe. Please remember that."

I nod, not really sure where he is going with this.

"Into The Wind rally is in the next few days, I want you with us."

Bomb... Dropped.

"Excuse me?"

No, he cannot be serious.

When they go to rallies, the clubhouse is empty and I get a break. Peace and quiet, where I'm left alone to enjoy some well-earned me-time.

"I'm sorry sweetheart but you need to trust me. You're coming to the rally."

Since when did he start to tell me what to do?

"Dad, are you sure I have to come?"

I honestly don't want to go.

THREE

CHAOS

STRETCHING my arms above my head, I make sure my muscles are ready for the long ride ahead. Grabbing my bag and roll up, I lock the door to my room and head to Church. Spotting Havoc, one of our prospects, I chuck my bag at him.

"Put that in the van," I tell him

He nods and heads outside. Havoc is a man of little words which is why he gets along with Psycho so well. The pair of them are both silent, brooding fuckers. I'm the last one in Church, that doesn't happen often but I'm the president so I can do what the fuck I like.

"Nice of you to join us," Riot smirks.

"Fucker," I mumble under my breath.

The arsehole just chuckles, always with the smart mouth, Riot.

"We all set for today?" I ask.

Nods greet me

CHAOS

"Van is packed, all bikes have full tanks and have been serviced. So, no one should be breaking down. I have a few bits in the van just in case, as you never know with you lot." Tracker says.

Being our Road Captain, he's in charge of all runs and making sure all our bikes are road safe and ready. Although it is also our responsibility to look after our own bikes. Any self-respecting biker looks after their bike, it's your pride and joy. A part of you.

"Good, are we all ready for the meeting with Tribal Bones?"

"I've been doing some digging, the one to watch is their VP Dyno. There is definitely something fishy regarding Voodoo disappearing. Before he vanished, he was in regular contact with his Prez, who is also his dad and other family members." Keys explains.

Keys has the ability to find anything and everything. Once you give him a task, he is like a dog with a bone, not giving up until every stone is unturned.

"From what I found on Dyno's computer…" Keys continues.

"Woah, hold up. You got your hands on Dyno's computer?" Dolla exclaims.

"Well not physically, I sent him a phishing email, so as soon as he opened the attachment, it set off a virus which gave me complete access."

Dolla looks shocked. I catch Mayhem's eyes and he smirks at me. We both know exactly what Keys is capable of.

"So, as I was saying, I checked his computer. Not much

on his emails but his search history was really interesting. He's been looking into how to keep a person hidden. I think Voodoo is alive but being held captive somewhere. Dyno wants the club, but he also wants to get into drugs."

"No way would Judge go for that or most of the others. They run a clean club for the most part," Riot joins in.

"Okay, Keys keep digging. Psycho, I want you to keep your eyes on Dyno during the meet, get a feel for him. Let's see what Judge has to say at the meeting. Right, if everything is ready, roll out," I say as I bring the gavel down, ending Church.

We all file out of the room and head for our bikes, it's a good ride to Yorkshire where Into The Wind bike rally is held. It's always a good weekend and one we look forward to every year. It's usually filled with great bands, drinking, and bonding with my brothers, plus making connections with other clubs. Reaching my bike, I nod to Twisted, our longest prospect. He should be patched in soon as long as he doesn't fuck anything up between then and now, he's got no worries. I'm not concerned, he's not fucked up so far, he runs our tattoo parlour Twisted Skin and is damn talented. Makes the club a lot of money and people come for miles to get a tattoo done by him. The waiting list is currently four months-long just to get a slot with him.

"All sorted and van packed?" I check.

"Yup, all ready to roll Prez."

"Mount up," I yell.

Straddling my bike, I watch as the others all get comfy on theirs. Once I hear all the engines start, I feel a sense of peace wash over me. There is something special about the sound a group of engines makes, almost like classical music. It soothes my soul and calms me. I raise my hand in the air and make a circle. Putting my bike into gear, I pull out through the gates and out onto the open road.

The ride to Yorkshire from our home in Eastford on the East coast of England is a glorious ride. Sweeping Dales and country views, plus amazing rolling country roads where you can really open the throttle and ride clear. The ride is a good five to six hours. We stop halfway to stretch our legs and grab some food at a service station. There is a lot of other clubs here when we pull in. Everyone is friendly, knowing we are all going to the same place.

After a bite to eat and catching up with other clubs, we hit the road again. Traffic isn't bad so we make good time and arrive before it gets dark. Finding a good camping site, we circle the bikes around where we will put the tents.

"Prospects, unload the van and get the tents set up," I holla.

Havoc and Killa start unloading the van, while Twisted starts to unpack everything. The three of them work well as a team and will make great brothers one day. I really need to remember to bring up patching Twisted at our next Church.

As the Prospects get to work, we head for a look round. There are hundreds of stalls selling everything to do with bikers as you can imagine. We wander around the stalls when I catch a glimpse of red hair. Long, wavy, red hair. I look back and it's gone.

"You okay Prez?" Riot asks as I've stopped dead in my tracks.

"Yeah, sorry," I reply and start moving again.

I catch Psycho's eyes, and he gives me a strange look. I'm not getting into one of his looks right now. He sees way more than he lets on, or we think he does. Nothing and I mean nothing gets past him. As we continue walking around the stalls, Tracker is eating half his weight in food. He currently has a cheeseburger in one hand and a hot dog in the other. Taking a bite from each as we walk along. That man loves his food, he is always eating and gets very excited at the thought of food. He's a human dustbin.

"Oh, Mexican food. I love Tacos," Trackers says as he bounces on his toes and quickly stuffs the hotdog into his face.

Seriously, how he eats like that and doesn't gain weight is beyond me. He eats like he should weigh fifty stone.

"Are you for real Tracker?"

"What? I'm still hungry," he exclaims as if we are all stupid.

"Dude, don't you think you have eaten enough already?" Riot asks as if it should already be obvious.

"I'm not full yet. I have a healthy appetite."

"Tracker, you have a very unhealthy appetite. Try eating a salad or vegetable once in a while," I advise.

We keep walking through the stalls and every so often I catch a flash of red hair and a figure made of dreams. I have no clue why but I'm drawn to the red and keep looking for her. I want to see her face better as I only saw a small glimpse before. I have this urgent need in my gut to see her.

Weirdest shit ever.

"You okay dude?" Mayhem asks as he slides up next to me.

"Yeah, why?"

"You're distracted, you keep looking around for something or someone. I mean you're always aware of your surroundings but not to this extent."

"Yeah, it's going to sound strange, like I'm losing my mind but earlier I caught sight of a redhead with a body made for sin. I keep seeing glimpses of red every so often. I'm drawn to her and I have this gut feeling. Fuck, I do sound like I'm losing my fucking mind," I sigh.

"Always trust your gut. If it's telling you this chick means something, then she does. I'll keep an eye out for her brother." He replies as he slaps me on the back and then joins the others.

I look over at Psycho, and he nods at me. Guess he heard our conversation, and he'll keep an eye out too. My gut has never let me down, so Mayhem is right, I need to listen to it.

FOUR

OLIVIA

I stand on the lot just near the doors to the clubhouse. My bag is in my hand and I'm watching everyone get ready to head out. I'm hoping that if I just stand here and not speak, I'll merge into the background, and they'll forget I'm here. Oh, how I wish that was my luck, but sadly it isn't.

"You're with me princess," Dyno snarls at me.

I stand my ground; there's no way am I getting on the back of his bike. I don't trust him with my safety normally, never mind on a bike. Getting on the back of a man's bike shows trust. You are trusting him to not know how to handle the beast and not lay it down.

Dyno wraps his hand tightly around the top of my arm, bruising it. I try to pull my arm back but this only causes him to tighten his grip and a whimper to fall from my lips.

"Do as your fucking told," he growls at me.

"Liv, you're with Archer," Dad shouts from his bike.

Dyno gives him an evil glare.

CHAOS

"She'll ride with me," he demands.

Archer and Foggy appear at my dad's side.

"Are you questioning our Prez about his own daughter?" Archer demands.

"She's not your Ol' lady, so you have no say. VP or not, the Prez's word is gold," Foggy backs him up.

Everyone is now staring at the scene they are making, waiting to see what move Dyno will make. He may be VP but what the Prez says goes. I notice Rattle and Lizard have slowly made their way closer to us, just in case they need to back Dyno up. The only person missing from the Wanker crew is Guts.

"Of course, not. We all know she's going to be my Ol' lady soon anyway." Dyno spits out.

"Liv honey, come here," Dad says, ignoring Dyno completely.

With another painful squeeze of my arm, causing me to hold in the whimper that wants to break free, Dyno finally lets me go with a hard push. Catching myself before I fall, Archer takes a step forward but dad stops him. I walk to dad and he wraps his arm around me.

"Trust me," he whispers into my hair as he kisses the side of my head.

Foggy takes my bag from me with a wink and loads into the van the prospect will be driving. I grab my helmet from dad and get ready to ride. It has been a long time since I've been on the back of a bike. I'm a daddy's girl and love riding. The free feeling of being on a bike. Wind therapy they call it. Once dad is ready at the front with Ford who is our Road captain, next to him, as he's plotted the route, my dad raises his fist into the air and makes a roll-out gesture. All the riders rev their engines and the power vibrates through the tarmac. Dad and Ford pull forward and everyone pulls out behind them in formation. A well-practiced synchronized move and we are off.

IT takes several hours to get to the rally, and we stop twice along the way. I make sure to stay away from Dyno and his Wanker crew. I stick close to my dad and those I know I can trust. Archer, Foggy, Trader, and Ford are close to my dad. They have always been kind to me and treated me with respect.

I miss my brother. Voodoo used to be the VP, but he's been missing for a few months and Dyno took over that spot. Once he did, he brought some of his own guys in. That is when everything went to shit, Dyno is not what the club needs and neither is his band of merry wankers. They are slowly destroying the club and trying to take over. I know in my gut that they have something to do with my brother's disappearance, no way would he just leave and not say goodbye to me.

We pull into a service station for our last stop. I am so ready to just get to the campground and away from Dyno. I can feel his eyes on me, burrowing into my back, making my skin crawl. I can't help going over his words in my head before we left.

No way will I ever be his Ol' Lady. I'd rather be dead than have him touch me.

I know he's pissed off that my dad overruled him and I'm riding behind Archer. Riding behind someone shows trust. I trust him, he handles his bike like it's an extension of his body. A skilled and knowledgeable rider. I wouldn't trust Dyno with anything, never mind my life.

"You hungry?" he asks me.

"No, I'm okay. I just want to get there," I tell him as we head inside.

"We'll be there soon enough. I'm going to grab a drink and some food. You okay or do you want to come with me?"

"Thanks, Arch but I'm going to freshen up. I'll meet you outside," I tell him with a smile.

Noting as I head for the ladies' room, that Dyno and his lackeys are at the food court, I feel safe enough being away from Archer and my dad. Using the facilities and freshening up, I head outside and wait near Archer's bike. Suddenly feel a finger slide down my arm. Whirling around, I come face to face with Dyno.

"Knew I would get you alone," he sneers.

I say nothing. A, *fuck you*, sits on the tip of my tongue but I manage to stop it from falling from my mouth. Sassing him wouldn't end well for me, I can't always help what falls from my mouth, it's like I have no filter.

"Nothing to say Princess?" he goads me.

"Archer and my dad will be back any minute."

"Still not going to save you, Princess. You will be mine

and so will Tribal Bones."

The cocky smirk on his face tells me he thinks he's got this all worked out and it will all end in his favour. He's delusional. My dad and the rest of them won't go down without a fight. He's underestimated my dad too many times before.

"Everything okay here?" Ford asks as he appears from around a lorry parked up near the bikes.

"Yeah man, just keeping our Princess here company," Dyno snaps back while giving Ford daggers.

"She's good," Ford replies as he presses his hand to the middle of my back and steers me away from Dyno and towards a group of picnic tables on the grassy area.

"You okay Liv?" he asks with concern in his voice.

"I am now, thanks, Ford."

"No worries, Liv, we've got you," he says, wrapping his arm around me and bringing me close to him.

It's comforting and I feel safe. We sit on one of the picnic tables while Ford devours his food and wait for the others to come back. Slowly everyone starts to meet back up.

"All, okay?" dad asks as he approaches me and Ford.

"Yeah, all good."

"You sure," Arches asks, looking concerned.

Nodding, I wrap my arms around my dad, and he cocoons me in his arms.

I'm such a daddy's girl but I can't help it. He's the greatest man I know.

"Love ya, baby girl," he whispers in my ear and kisses

the top of my head.

"Love ya too dad," I whisper back, snuggling further into him.

"Let's hit the road," Dyno roars, breaking the moment.

Pathetic, jealous fucker.

He hates when my dad shows me affection, it always causes him to be extra nasty. I have no clue why. Guess he's just that weird and twisted. We head for the bikes and mount up. Once again, we will pull out in formation and make our way on the last part of our journey.

It only takes us about another hour or so before we are in the queue to get into the campground. Finding a good spot, the prospects start to set up camp. The rally is huge with thousands of clubs and bikers attending. Filling several fields with tents and then another couple of fields are filled with food and drinks vendors. The stalls are selling everything a biker could wish for, a huge stage for the bands set to play, plus even a small funfair with rides for the kids that have come along.

"Come on Liv, let's go for a walk around," Dad says.

Nodding, I fall in beside him and Archer throws his arm around my shoulders. I hear the growl from behind us as we walk away. Knowing full well that growl came from Dyno, I can't help the smirk that forms on my face.

Serves the twat right.

We walk around the stalls and stop every so often to look closer at certain ones. I buy a new bracelet from one stall and I spot a lovely leather bag on another. Archer gives me a look when I put the beautiful handmade shoulder bag in a deep green leather back.

"Why aren't you getting it?" he asks.

"It's handmade and beautiful. With a beautiful price tag to match," I tell him.

No way can I afford it. Dyno is meant to give me money as I clean the clubhouse and keep it for brothers, but he doesn't always give it to me and when he does, it's not always the right amount. I move to the next stall where dad is looking at some riding gloves. Helping him choose a pair, I don't notice Archer is missing until he pops up next to me and hands me a bag.

"What's this?" I ask.

"Present," he smirks

Shaking my head, I open the bag and pull out the green leather shoulder bag, I was looking at. I stroke the soft leather and slowly raise my head to look at him.

"Thank you," I say in a soft voice.

"Welcome Angel."

Archer has always been like a brother to me. He's my brother's best friend, and they have been close since school. He has always treated me more like his little sister. We carry on walking through the stalls and I catch sight of the most beautiful man I have ever seen. He makes me stop dead in my tracks. His dark hair is cut close to his head and his sunglasses sit perfectly on his face. He has this aura around him that shows he's a badass without actually doing anything.

I can't stop staring at him and it's as if he feels me staring, that he starts to look my way. I quickly get a hold of myself and turn away, hurrying to catch up with dad and

Archer. As we continue to walk through the stalls, we stop to get food, because this bunch never stops eating, I keep catching a glimpse of him. It's like I'm drawn to him which is strange. I've never felt drawn to anyone before, never mind someone I've not spoken to or seen up close.

Shaking my head, I try to get rid of the thoughts I'm having about a total stranger.

What the hell is wrong with me?

I focus on the rest of the stalls, even though I keep catching little bits of the man, but I never come face to face with him.

FIVE

CHAOS

PUSHING the redhead out my mind, for now, we spend the rest of the evening relaxing at the camp and getting ready for our meeting with Tribal Bones MC. I am not looking forward to the meeting. Don't get me wrong; I like Judge and have respect for him as a friend of my dad's but something is very wrong within his MC right now. My gut is screaming at me to be careful. It's never led me wrong yet, so I'm going to pay attention.

"Are you ready for the meeting?" Mayhem asks from beside me.

"Yeah, need to be our game," I warn him.

"Your gut talking to you again?" he smirks.

"Fucker. Yeah, it is, so be on the lookout."

I watch the brothers mess around and relax. The prospects built a fire in the middle of the tents, which is currently blazing away. Drinks around being passed around, followed by the odd joint or two. The air is filled with the scent of burning wood and weed. I relax back in my chair and take a swig of my beer. Sitting here with my brothers makes me feel humble. I honestly feel honoured to call these idiots my family, and we are a family.

Regardless of what people may think of us, loyalty is everything. I've known some of my brothers since school, growing up with Mayhem and Psycho, we have a bond forged in history. We met Riot in our teens, and he fits perfectly into our little group. The four of us are close, I would do anything for them, and they would do the same for me. That includes their families.

Mayhem's son Logan and his folks mean the world to me. I love being Logan's uncle and spoiling him every chance I get. He's only four right now but I'm already planning a Prospect in training cut for his fifth birthday. Plus, we need to get that kid on a bike. He's the future of this club.

"Twist is in place," Psycho says as he drops down in the chair on the other side of Mayhem and me.

"Good. How are you feeling about the meet?" Mayhem asks him.

"Something's not right," Psycho replies.

"Yeah, Prez's gut is going off too," Mayhem replies.

"Should always listen to his gut."

"Oi you fuckers, I'm sat here," I growl, getting sick of them talking over me like I'm not fucking sat here. The pair of them just laugh.

"We ready?" Riot asks joining us.

"Let's get this over with," I say, standing from my seat.

Psycho and Mayhem join me as we all start heading for

the meeting point that was previously arranged. As we get closer, Psycho fades into the shadows, while Mayhem and Riot flank me at either side. I spot Judge, his Wanker of a VP Dyno, and Archer, his Sergeant At Arms waiting for us.

"Judge," I greet him, shaking his hand.

"Chaos, good to see you son. How have you been?" he asks.

"Good," I reply shortly.

He's looking a little nervous and doesn't seem to be his usual self. I've known this man for years and the strange vibe he's giving off is causing me to be a little concerned.

"All good with you?"

"Yeah, all good," he says but his eyes say something different.

"Right, let's get to business," Dyno interrupts.

I give him an unimpressed look.

Disrespectful fucker.

"Alright Dyno, you in a rush?" Mayhem asks, clearly as unimpressed with him as me.

"Just want to get this over with, shit to do," he growls back.

I'm sick of this fucker already and I have no tolerance for disrespect, which is what he's showing not only us but his own club too right now.

"Wanna show a little fucking respect. Wouldn't want to damage a long partnership now, would you?" I growl back at him.

"Dyno, fucking step back," Judge snaps at him.

Clearly, his own Prez has had enough too. Archer moves

a little closer to his Prez but not in a stance to protect him from us, no. This is a stance to protect his Prez from Dyno. Proving all is not good inside Tribal Bones MC at all. Dyno takes a step back, but by the look on his face, he isn't happy.

"Sorry Chaos. Here is the final payment." Judge says handing me an envelope.

I hand it off to Mayhem to check.

"Thanks, Judge, don't usually meet like this to collect payment," I ask, intrigued as to why he wanted to meet.

"I know but as Mayhem will find out I'm a little short this month," he confesses.

I look to Mayhem who nods as he finishes checking the payment.

"About twenty thousand short," Mayhem advises.

"Judge, you want to explain this?" I ask.

"I've never been short before Chaos and this is the final payment. The club is struggling financially at the moment. I will get you the extra twenty thousand, I just need a little extra time."

I look at Mayhem who is staring at Judge with a very unhappy look on his face. My face matches his and so does Riot's. We run a business, not a charity. We're not usually in the business of giving people second chances but I might consider it due to our history, however, twenty thousand is a lot to be short.

"Twenty thousand is a lot, Judge."

"I know Chaos, I just need a little more time. What do you say I give you collateral for it?"

Okay, now he has my attention. What could he possibly offer me that's worth twenty thousand or more? It's at that moment Psycho appears next to me with a strange look on his face.

"What's the collateral?" Psycho asks.

Judge turns to Archer and nods and he takes his phone out and sends a text.

"Judge, what the fuck is going on?" I demand, getting really pissed off with this now.

It's a few minutes later, that Ford, a member of Tribal Bones, appears with the shock of my life. There stood with him, is the redhead that I've been seeing everywhere today.

"Explain, now," I bark out.

"Chaos, this is my daughter Olivia. I want you to accept her as collateral."

"The fuck?" I say at the same time as Olivia turns and exclaims the same thing.

"No way my Ol' lady is going anywhere," Dyno growls and reaches out to grab her.

Without even thinking I move forward, wrapping my arm around her waist and pulling her to me before Dyno can touch her.

"She is not your Ol' lady. I've told you many times before Dyno," Judge throws back at him.

"Rather chop my arm off than be his Ol' lady," Olivia mutters under her breath, thinking no one can hear her, but I did and it causes me to chuckle.

Dyno starts to head for Judge but Archer steps in and Riot steps forward, so he's nearly in front of me and Olivia. Psycho and Mayhem close ranks around us, forming a protective shield of sorts. I feel her stiffen in my arms and

CHAOS

I don't want her to feel scared.

"It's okay, we won't let him hurt you," I try to reassure her.

"It's not me I'm worried about. I don't want him hurting my dad," she whispers back.

"Archer and Ford have him covered," I tell her.

At that, she relaxes slightly against me. Stroking her arm, I move her behind me so she's protected. I tap Psycho and Mayhem on the shoulders to step aside. They move to the side but also step back so they are covering Olivia too.

"Judge, seriously what the fuck?" I demand.

"I know Chaos. This is not how we normally do business."

"Too fucking right, it's not normally how we do business. We don't deal in skin," I tell him.

"Don't worry, you'll have your money. Hand Liv back," Dyno demands.

I'm so sick of this guy already. He needs to learn his place, showing no fucking respect for me or his own Prez. I am about to lose my head with him if he doesn't back off.

"Won't warn you again Dyno, show some fucking respect. I am speaking with your President, not you. This doesn't concern you. Judge has already said she's not your Ol' lady and never will be. Clearly, you've not claimed her at Church or if you have it didn't pass. So, you need to back the fuck off and not stick your nose where it doesn't belong," I spit back at him.

Turning to look at Judge, I see the look in his eyes. He's begging me to take her. This really isn't something we would normally do but my gut is telling me I need to. He's not selling her but more asking us to keep her safe. I feel a tap on my leg and look to Psycho. He nods ever so slightly so only I can see it. Guess he's seeing the same as me. This is a father protecting his daughter. He knows the Road Wreckers MC hates people who abuse women and children. If I thought anyone in my club was mistreating their Ol' lady or children, not only would they be stripped of their patch, but they would be meeting their maker too. Sick twisted fuckers like that never learn their lesson.

"Okay, we will take Olivia, and she will be safe with us," I assure him.

I feel her stiffen behind me, so I reach back and grip her hip with my hand. Stroking my thumb over the small sliver of skin showing between her top and jeans, hoping this reassures her that I'm doing this for the right reasons. Dyno clearly still pissed, lunges for Judge. Before any of Tribal Bones can react, Psycho has knocked the fucker out.

"Thank you," Archer says to Psycho, who only nods in return.

Jesus this is turning into a shit show fast.

"We need to get out of here." Riot says.

Nodding, I agree and turn and wrap my arm back around Olivia's waist, holding her to me. Thankfully she doesn't try to move away. She's watching Dyno try to sit up and more Tribal Bones making their way towards us.

"Judge, this concludes our business. Do you have Olivia's things?"

He nods and takes the bag from a prospect, he steps towards us, handing me it. Judge then pulls Olivia into his arms and whispers in her ear. Her body shakes a little like she's crying. The thought of her upset makes me want to pull her into my arms and make it all better for her.

Seriously, what the actual fuck.

I've never had this reaction to a woman before. Especially one I haven't said more than a handful of words to. This is not normal, even for me, but I can't help myself from wanting to touch her and needing her to be within reach.

"We need to go," Psycho says, clearing his throat.

Clearly as uncomfortable as me right now, I nod and put my hand on Olivia's shoulder.

"Sorry to break this up, but we got to go," I say as softly as possible.

Olivia and her dad separate and she wipes under her eyes but comes back to stand next to me, causing a small smile to cross my face.

Jesus, she is perfect, with a little sass if her comment earlier is anything to go by.

"You look after my little girl and I'll be in touch," Judge warns before he turns and walks away.

"Let's move quickly," Riot orders and we all start moving back to camp.

SIX

OLIVIA

THIS is not happening. For fuck's sake, this cannot be my life. What have I done in a former life to have to deal with all this crap? I'm not a bad person. I try hard to be nice to people. So why can't for once in my life things just go my way? I don't think I'm asking for a lot, to be honest. Yes, I may have a little sass but that doesn't make me a bad person. Yet here I am standing with my dad while he uses me as collateral for the club's debt. He is selling me by the sounds of it. My own dad, selling me.

My heart is breaking. How can he do this to me? I'm his daughter, he's meant to love and protect me. Not use me like this. If someone had told me this would happen, I would have laughed in their faces and told them they were crazy.

Clearly, I'm the crazy one. What's even worse is the guy whose dad selling me to is the guy I spotted at the stalls earlier. Up close, he's even more beautiful than I thought he was. He has the most piercing blue eyes and this pure masculine aurora that is calling to me.

The man my dad refers to as Chaos has his eyes firmly fixed on me. It's as if he can see right through into my soul. Just him staring at me with that look in his eye, makes me want to bear my soul and every dark, hidden secret I ever had. They are now arguing over whatever is being said. Their words don't seem to be registering with my brain, all I see is him. It's like I'm in some sort of fog. Suddenly my dad's words register the same time as they hit Chaos

"The fuck?" I say at the same time as Chaos.

"No way my Ol' lady is going anywhere" Dyno growls.

Suddenly he's lunging for me, within a second, Chaos moves gracefully and with the speed of a jungle animal. His arm wraps around my waist and I'm pulled into him. He protects me from me Dyno, who is now aiming for my dad. I can hear him shouting about me being his Ol' lady.

"Rather chop my arm off than be his Ol' lady," I mumble under my breath, unable to help myself. I can feel Chaos's muscles move as he chuckles.

Shit, clearly, I didn't say that as quietly as I thought I did.

I notice Dyno is still trying to reach my dad, causing my body to stiffen, I don't want my dad hurt.

"It's okay, we won't let him hurt you," he whispers to me.

"Not me I'm worried about. I don't want him hurting my dad," I whisper back.

"Archer and Ford have him covered." He tells me and I relax into him, clinging onto his cut.

I can hear the shouting going back and forth between

them but I keep my head buried in his back. I somehow feel like he will protect me and I'm safe with him. I can't explain why I know this but I do. However, that knowledge doesn't stop my body from reacting to what he announces next.

"Okay, we will take Olivia, and she will be safe with us," he tells my dad, authority in his voice.

As my body tenses back up, Chaos moves his hand to my hip and strokes the small slice of skin showing. Just the tip of his thumb stroking my skin sends an electric current through me. He moves me in front of him and I can see Dyno laying on the ground, and I'm unable to help the small smirk that crosses my lips.

Serves the twat right.

Dad pulls me into his arms as a prospect hands Chaos my bag.

"I know this doesn't make sense and you probably hate me but please Angel, trust me. This is to keep you safe and because I love you more than anything. Please don't hate me," dad whispers in my ear.

"I don't hate you. Yes, I'm confused. You just sold me but if you're asking me to trust you then of course I do. I love you, daddy."

Unable to keep the tears anyway any longer, they fall down my cheeks as I cling to my dad.

"I love you, Angel," he tells me, kissing my head.

I can only nod, as I'm unable to speak.

"We need to go," someone says.

I feel a hand on my shoulder, gently pulling me away

from my dad.

"Sorry to break this up, but we got to go," Chaos says in a soft voice.

I step back and wipe the tears from my eyes. Once I've got myself together, I step back to Chaos's side.

"You look after my little girl and I'll be in touch," Dad says before he turns and walks away.

"Let's move quickly," another man says.

We all turn and start heading to the campground. Chaos is in front of me and his men are surrounding us, forming a protective ring. We get a little way away and another man appears out of nowhere and joins us. I have a death grip on the back of Chaos's cut, clinging to him for dear life. I wonder what type of men they are and what they expect from me. The unknown is making me wary to trust them too much, but then again, the way they surround me, offering protection, they can't be all bad, right? I guess only time will tell.

I look up at the man on my right, he has his hair long on top and shaved on the sides. He must feel me looking at him as he turns to look at me. He has the most beautiful green eyes I have ever seen. He gives me a wink with a cheeky smile. I can't help but smile back at him as he's putting me at ease. We reach a circle of tents with a fire going in the middle.

"This is my tent, why don't you get some rest, while I talk to my brothers. You're safe here with us Olivia." Chaos tells me while running his hands up and down my arms.

"Thank you," I say and crawl into the tent we stopped in front of.

I lay down and try to process what has happened tonight. I can hear men's voices but not what they are saying so they must have moved away from the tents a little. The voices are gentle and soothing, and before I know it, I feel myself drifting off to sleep.

I'M not sure how long I'm asleep when I feel someone in the tent, slowly opening my eyes, I see Chaos looking through a bag. I watch him for a few minutes, his arms flex as he rummaged through his things. The short sleeve of his t-shirt is wrapped tightly around his arm muscles.

Yeah, I know. Sorry I have a bit of a thing for strong, muscular arms.

He's crouched down on his hunches and his thigh muscles strain as they keep him upright, he then looks over at me.

"Sorry, I didn't mean to wake you."

"That's okay. Do you want your tent back?" I say as I start to leave.

"No, you stay there. I'll sleep outside. It's safer for you here, but if you need anything, I'll just be outside plus a couple of prospects are taking turns to stand guard," he says as he grabs a rolled-up sleeping bag.

"Are you sure? I don't want to put you out."

"Darlin, you're not putting me out. Stay in the tent, I'll

be outside. You need to sleep as we're leaving first thing in the morning," he warns as he turns and leaves the tent.

I lay back down and curl up with the pillow. It smells of aftershave, a manly one which suits him, more of a musky scent. I snuggle the pillow and let the smell help me relax and drift back off to sleep.

IT'S early the next morning and I can hear a lot of activity going on outside the tent. I stretch and work the kinks out of my muscles and slowly make my way outside.

"Morning sleepyhead," the dark-haired man from yesterday greets me.

"Morning," I reply shyly.

"Don't be shy, you're good now. I'm Riot, the Sergeant At Arms for this bunch of delinquents," he says making me laugh.

"Yeah, and he's the biggest delinquent out of all of us," another replies.

Riot laughs and flicks the finger at him.

"I'm Mayhem sweetheart, VP," he says but I can't stop looking at his lovely thick hair, which is a gorgeous chestnut colour.

"Don't let our Prez catching you giving VP the eye," Riot chuckles, causing me to duck my head down so I'm looking at the ground

"Fucker, now you've made her feel awkward," Mayhem says, punching Riot in the arm.

"Ignore me, Olivia, I'm only teasing," Riot assures me.

I smile at the easy banter between them. It used to be like this in my dad's club but since Dyno joined and then introduced his Wanker crew, it's not been the same.

I miss the family we used to be.

SEVEN

CHAOS

I can see Riot and Mayhem talking to Olivia. They seem to have her smiling, which is good. I want her to be relaxed around the brothers, for her to feel at ease.

Don't ask me why, because I have no clue.

She draws me in, I can't keep my eyes off her. I have this need to keep her in my sights.

Fuck, I need to get a grip.

"Are we nearly ready to head out?" Tracker asks.

"Yeah, just my tent to pack away now that Olivia is up," I tell him

"I'll get the prospects on it," he nods and moves off to where the prospects are loading the van.

Riot and Mayhem are still stood talking to Olivia, so I grab the bottle of water and breakfast sandwich I got her, and start heading their way.

"Morning, you sleep, okay?" I ask as I get closer to them.

"Like a baby Prez," Riot answers.

"Not you, fuck face," I tell him with a roll of my eyes.

Olivia giggles as Riot lets out a massive belly laugh. Her giggle brings a smile to my face. It's an amazing sound and lights up her whole face, she really needs to laugh and smile more.

"Here, I got you these," I say, handing her the sandwich and drink.

"Thank you," she says as she takes them and sits down at the picnic bench that's close by.

I leave her to it and grab her bag plus mine out of the tent, making sure everything is packed. Twisted comes and starts to pack my tent and sleeping bag away, ready to put in the van.

"Do you need to freshen up once you've eaten?" I ask her.

"Yes please, if it's not too much trouble."

"Of course, not. Get freshened up as soon as you've finished breakfast, but make sure you let one of us know you're heading to the bathrooms," I warn her.

"Why?" she asks, with an unsure look on her face.

"Nothing to worry about Olivia, just want to make sure you're safe. Especially after last night," I reassure her.

"Okay, thank you" she replies and continues to pick at her sandwich.

"You're not hungry?"

"Sorry, I appreciate you getting me breakfast," she says, with a timid voice.

I crouch down in front of her and take her hands in mine. Rubbing my thumbs across the tops of her hands, they feel perfect in mine, like they are meant to be there.

"If you are not hungry just say. You can be yourself around us, I guess you've had to hide yourself a little in front of Dyno. Not with us though. I caught a glimpse of your sass and fire last night, don't be afraid to be yourself," I tell her, hoping she understands that we aren't going to hurt her.

"Thank you for being so kind. It has all just been a lot to deal with. I mean my dad sold me," Her voice hitches at the end, as her emotions get the better of her.

Unable to stop myself from touching her, I wrap my arms around her and pull her into my chest. Running my hand over her head, I hold her tight as she cries. The sound of her gut-wrenching sobs hits me right in the chest. I'd do anything to make this right for her.

"She okay," Riot says as he sits on the chair next to her and rubs his hand up and down her back.

Clearly, I'm not the only one who Olivia has managed to get under her spell. I notice Mayhem and Psycho have moved closer to check she's okay. Twister appears with a bottle of water and some tissues.

Jesus, it's like the whole club is looking out for her.

A feeling of pride fills me at how my brothers instantly have my back and hers too, as they've noticed I have feelings for her.

"You okay sweetheart?" I ask her.

"Yeah, I'm so sorry for crying on you," she says as she pulls back and gets herself together, and looking embarrassed at the brothers around us seeing her like this.

"Now there is no need to be shy. If you need to cry then

let it all out." Riot says with a smirk on his face and a wink.

Jesus, if he did like women the rest of us would be fucked.

Women love him and he puts them at ease. It helps that he's a big old flirt too, can't help himself.

"Sorry to break this up, but we need to head off shortly. Everything is packed except Olivia's bag," Tracker says as he comes to join us with Dolla, both giving Olivia reassuring, friendly smiles.

"You want to get freshened up, and then we can go?" I ask her.

She nods and starts to collect her bag. Riot gives me a chin lift to let me know he'll take her. I watch him link arms with her and lead her to the bathrooms. I use the word bathrooms but that's being generous, these are Portaloos and nothing special. Just basic plastic toilets but some are bigger with large sinks in them and space to get cleaned up. Hopefully this early into the rally, they should still be clean enough. I set about making sure everything is packed as it should be and nothing is left behind. I check in with Tracker about the plan for the trip home.

"Is Olivia riding with you or in the van?" Tracker asks.

"Not sure to be honest, I'll ask her which she would feel more comfortable doing."

"Okay, my plan is to go straight home. Maybe only one-stop if we need to but otherwise, we need to get home where we are most secure. From what Riot and Psycho said about the meeting, we need to keep an eye on Dyno. Man is Crazy."

"You're not wrong. Dyno is losing the plot. Even as VP

you don't go against your Prez, not like he did. Screaming about Olivia being his Ol' lady, she isn't shit to him."

"She going to be something to you?" He asks with a smirk.

"Cheeky fucker, we will see," I say as she comes back, laughing with Riot.

I can't help myself from watching her as she throws her head back and laughs at something he says to her. Her laugh and smile light up her entire face, no one can help smiling when she gives you that smile of hers. I notice Psycho watching and even that miserable, brooding arsehole, has a slight smile watching Olivia and Riot. I want to know what Riot has said that is so funny. Part of me wants her smiles just for myself.

Jealous bastard already and she's not even mine, yet.

"Are we all ready to go?" I ask as they get closer to me.

"Yes, all ready," she says as I reach and take the bag from her hand.

Our fingers brush against each other and I feel a spark shoot through me. We stay just as we are, the bag between us, our fingers touching on the handle, just staring at each other. Clearly, she felt the same spark that I did, this woman is messing with my feelings without even trying. It's as if she has no clue the effect, she is having not only on me but my brothers too. They all seem to have taken to her quickly.

"Erm, do you want to ride in the van or on my bike?" I ask, clearing my throat as I recover.

"I don't want to put anyone out. I can ride in the van if it is easier," her voice is small like she is unsure of herself.

"Do you like riding?" I ask, praying she says yes.

The thought of her wrapped around me as we ride down the motorway, wind around us. Just the feeling of her arms around me and her legs resting along mine, I need to know what that feels like. I want her to put her trust in me to keep her safe, not just from Dyno but on my bike too.

"I love to ride. Dad used to take me out when I was younger and I've been a few times with some of the brothers."

The image of her on another man's bike fills me with jealousy. I have no right to be jealous, I didn't know her then but I want to be her one and only.

Jesus, if this carries on, she's going to have my balls before I can get her to be mine. I seriously need to pull myself together.

"Then you are more than welcome to ride with me Olivia if you would like?" I quickly add.

"I would like that, Chaos."

Jesus, fuck, shit.

The way my name sounds coming from her plump lips has my cocking going hard in a second. I have to swallow a few times and count the players of the nineteen sixty-six World cup to make my cock go down a little. Can't be riding with cock hard as steel, while she is clinging to me.

"Okay then, let's hit the road," I shout.

I pass Olivia's bag off to Twisted to put in the van. She looks sexy as fuck in tight, light, denim jeans, that fit her like a glove. A Harley-Davidson t-shirt, which again shows off her assets without being slutty, a deep purple leather jacket, and black riding boots. She is the picture of beautiful biker chick chic. We reach my bike and I hand her the spare helmet I got ready, hoping she would agree to ride with me. I mount my bike and put my helmet on. Steadying the bike between my thighs, I tap the seat behind me.

"Get on babes."

Her smile gets even bigger than I thought possible, as she places her hand on my shoulder to help her up and swings her leg over the seat. I watch her in my wing mirror, she makes it look so graceful and effortless as she sits down behind me, gripping the side of my cut. I grab her legs and pull her forward so she's flush against me and then wrap her arms around my waist. Tapping her hand in reassurance. I raise my hand in the air and make a circle with my finger. I hear all the bikes start up behind me and Tracker is next to me, as he will take the lead as Road Captain.

As the engines all roar to life, I feel Olivia shake behind me. I look in the wing mirror to check she's okay. She has another huge grin on her face. Guess it was a good shiver. As one, we all move forward and start to make our way through the camp to get to the main road out of the campground. As we're slowly rolling through, I feel Olivia tap my left side, I look to check she's okay and catch why she tapped me. Over to the far left is Dyno, standing glaring at us with a few members of Tribal Bones. I glare back at him while my hand moves to her leg, giving her a reassuring squeeze. Dyno's glare goes to one of murder once he notices. I smirk at him as we ride on.

Fuck the prick.

We make it to the main road and head out on our way. We ride for a good few hours, before pulling into a service station. I'm getting too old for these long rides. My muscles are stiff and I awkwardly dismount my bike after Olivia hopes off.

How in the hell is she moving around like that after being on the bike for so long?

"You, okay?" she asks me as I try to stretch the aches out of my muscles.

"Yeah, body is not what it used to me. Long rides make my muscles hurt," I tell her, feeling fucking old.

I'm only thirty-seven years old but I might as well be seventy-three by the way my muscles are. I definitely need to start working out more. I'm not getting any younger and I need to start taking better care of myself.

"None of us are as young as we used to be, especially Prez," Riot says as he comes up, slings his arm around Olivia's shoulders, guiding her into the service station.

"Cheeky fucker," I mumble at him.

His loud laugh is all I get back.

EIGHT

OLIVIA

I love the easy banter between the brothers. Riot teasing Chaos about his age, makes me chuckle. Guess Chaos is the oldest of the group. Even if they all look young and fit, I notice a few of them moving a little slower, stretching out their muscles after several hours on the bikes. This is where yoga comes in handy for me. It keeps my muscles nice and stretched, so long rides don't bother me as much.

"Riot, don't be mean," I tell him as he drops his arm across my shoulders as we walk into the service station.

"Sticking up for Prez already. You wound me, Livie. Thought I was your favourite," he says sticking his lip out.

"God you really are a flirt. Just can't help yourself, can you?" I ask with a giggle.

"Can't help being this brilliant," he replies, heading for the food court.

Laughing, I follow along as I'm getting hungry. After all of us got some food, which Chaos kindly, without giving me a choice, paid for, we hit the bathrooms. I did my business and freshened up a little. Leaving the ladies, I found all the guys waiting outside for me.

"Come on Sweetpea. Let's hit the road; I want to get home," Chaos says, guiding me back outside.

I love the little nickname. He's been using terms of endearment for me a lot more and I find myself liking it. I get that might not make me a feminist but there is more to being one. A pet name makes me feel treasured and loved. Which is an odd feeling, considering I've only known Chaos and his brothers, not even a full day, but each of them has been so kind and welcoming. None of them have made me feel unsafe or scared to be around them. No one has barked an order at me.

However, we are not at the clubhouse yet. I'm still unsure of what my role will be once we do get there. Am I to be a club girl? No way could I sleep around like that. I mean more power to the girls who can but it's just not for me. Do they expect me to clean and fetch for them as Dyno did? I don't want to be someone else's slave. I'm brought out of my musing when Chaos touches my shoulder. I hadn't noticed we'd reached the bikes as I'd been quiet as we crossed the car park.

"You okay," he asks, concern written across his face.

"I'm sorry, I zoned out there for a moment," I explain, dropping my chin.

"Hey, don't hide from me. I can hear your brain working, do you have some questions?" he asks, as he lightly grips my chin and lifts my head up until I'm looking into his handsome face and beautiful blue eyes.

"Be honest with me" he demands, seeing right through me and knowing I didn't want to tell him what I was thinking.

"I don't know what you expect from me once we get back to your clubhouse. Am I to be a club girl or keep the clubhouse and brothers?" I finally ask.

"How do you mean keep the clubhouse and brothers, Sweetpea?"

"Well, my dad used to ask that I keep the clubhouse clean and stock the kitchen. Maybe do some cooking now and then as the brothers struggled to boil water, plus make sure the bar was stocked too. Dyno also made me clean the full clubhouse including bathrooms and the brother's room and do anything else he deemed a woman's job."

"So basically, be is fucking slave?" the anger in Chaos' voice makes me step back.

Within seconds Riot was beside me with his arms around me, plus Mayhem and psycho are standing next to Chaos but more so they were in front of him, shielding me.

"What the fuck Chaos, take it down several notches. You're scaring Liv," Mayhem tells him.

His face instantly changes from one of anger to regret.

"Sweetpea I would never hurt you. If I ever hurt you, Riot and Psycho have permission to beat the shit out of me. I'm so sorry I scared you. RWMC treasures women and treats them with respect. We do not treat them as slaves. The fact your dad allowed his VP and his brothers to treat you as if you were a fucking slave like that, enrages me," Chaos says with remorse and guilt in his voice. He looks so sincere when he says this, that I want to believe him.

"Are you fucking joking me? They treated you as a slave?" Riot asks as Mayhem also looks at me. I notice Psycho is also watching me with anger in his eyes.

"Yes, Dyno made me scrub the bathrooms and toilets, plus the brothers' rooms., Well, only a few brothers that I refer to as the Wanker crew."

This gets them laughing, even Psycho chuckles.

"Wanker crew. I like it Liv," Mayhem chuckles as Riot is hanging off me laughing.

"You're a hoot Liv baby," Riot finally says when he stops laughing.

"Who is part of the Wanker crew?" Psycho asks.

"Well Dyno is head Wanker, then there is Rattle who is one of the Enforcers but Dyno pushed for that, and Guts and Lizard. Guts is the worse one, to be honest, I avoid him as much as possible."

Chaos comes towards me slowly like I'm a scared animal and might bolt any moment. The others step back to give us a little privacy.

"Sweetpea, I am so sorry I scared you. Please know I would never raise my hand to you in anger."

He looks so guilty and hurt that I thought he would hurt me, it makes my stomach sink. This man and his brothers have done nothing but show me kindness, and yet I keep comparing them to the Wanker crew.

"I'm sorry," I say

"No Olivia, I'm the one who is sorry. You don't have to apologise for your feelings. This is the way you feel and you should never apologise for that. I just need to do better at showing you we're the good guys. That I'm a good guy."

"You've already shown me that you and your club are the good guys. Sadly, old habits die hard, but I'll to do better" I reassure him. I hate to think my actions or reactions have caused him or the others to think they are bad guys.

"Olivia, Sweetpea. Please don't apologise for reacting the way you do. The more you are around us all, the more comfortable you will be. Now let's get back on the road," he says as he guides me back to the bikes.

Getting settled behind him, we hit the road. I love the feeling of being on the bike behind Chaos. Watching him control the bike with such power is making me a little hot. He is simply not just riding the bike. The bike has become an extension of himself and does this with such ease that it is hard not to feel safe with him.

The last part of the ride back to the clubhouse takes a few hours and finally we are pulling into the front of the clubhouse. Chaos taps my leg, which is biker speak for its time to get off. Dismounting, my muscles scream at me. I move to Chaos can walk the bike backwards into his spot. I take a moment to stretch my muscles, reaching as high as I can and then bending to touch my toes., then a few yoga stretches. Once I stand back up, I notice all of them are sitting on their bikes, just watching me stretch. I can't stop the blush that creeps over my face.

"Fuck Liv baby, you need to teach me to bend like that," Riot calls out, while making a few rude gestures

The others groan and roll their eyes at his antics as they

all dismount the bikes. We move as a group towards to the clubhouse and that's when I get my first clear view of the building. It is a rather large old red brick warehouse, with a large garage attached. Looking around I can the area is enclosed with a tall wire fence, keeping everything secure. Looking around I realise I'm lagging behind and rush to keep up as everyone files through the door and inside the clubhouse. Just as we enter the door, the scraping of crawls on the floor and loud barks can be heard. A few seconds later, two rather large Rottweilers appear, heading straight for Chaos. I take a step back as an arm comes around my shoulders.

"Don't scared. They make look fierce but trust me they are soft teddies really. Spend more time licking air as if they are fucking lizards," Riot chuckles in my ear.

Chaos is now knelt on the floor with both dogs fussing over him, trying to what looks like lick him to death. Maybe Riot is right.

"Liv Sweetpea, meet my babies, this is Raze and King," Chaos says, holding is hand out for me to take.

He gives me a reassuring smile as a place my hand in his and kneel next to him. Both dogs are sitting looking at me with their heads tilted, staring intently at me, judging me. I slowly reach my hands out for each of them to smell.

"Boys, this Liv," Chaos says.

Both dogs slowly smell my hand then a second later I'm laid on my looking at the ceiling while they give me, what I think might the seal of approval by also trying to lick me to death. I can't help the giggle that bursts free.

CHAOS

"Okay boys, enough," shouts Chaos as the dogs lets me up and I finally get a look around the clubhouse.

The inside is not what I thought it would be. It opens into a main commons area which is dotted with large leather sofas with solid coffee tables in front of them, then bar style tables and chairs mixed in. The bar again is solid wood and takes up the back wall with high stools lined up in front of it. A swing door to the right of the bar looks like it might lead to a kitchen area. To the left is large arched opened which I'm not where it leads. The walls are painted a warm grey with black and white old photos hanging of what looks like past members and gatherings. Mixed in with photos are old fashioned Harley Davidson and Indian bike memorabilia.

As I'm looking around the prospects have brought peoples person bags inside.

"Come on Sweetpea, I'll show you where you can freshen up." Chaos says as he guides me down the corridor which is lined with what look like offices and then up some stairs.

The dogs are trotting behind us. We continue down a corridor and stop at door on the right towards the bottom. Chaos unlocked the door and lets us in. The room is bright, with a large window overlooking the front of building. The room is set out like a living space, there is large grey comfy looking sofa facing a large TV and entertainment centre. Typical man, the TV is massive.

A lovely natural wood coffee table sits between the sofa and the TV unit. At the side is a large cosy chair which matches the sofa. A small side table sits between the sofa and chair with a lamp sitting on it. Over on the other side is a kitchen area. It looks modern with white units and plenty of counter space, a cooker and hob with built in microwave and plus an island separating it from the main living space, with stool tucked under to make a breakfast bar. The space is really clean but lacks that homely touch. The dogs push past me and drop down on the rug as if we are now boring them.

"This is my space, the kitchen you can see, the door over there is a bathroom and the other next to it is my bedroom. I'm really sorry but we don't have any spare rooms at the moment so you can have mine," he tells me.

Looking over to where he points, on the walls of the TV unit is two doors, one open, showing the bathroom and another closed, which must be the bedroom.

"Where will you sleep?" I ask following him into the bedroom with my bag still in my hand.

The bedroom is very male. A huge bedroom fills the room, with dark grey bedding and a black blanket laid across the bottom. A dresser is at the bottom of the bed, against the wall with another TV on it. The windows again are big and letting lots of light in. The other wall is filled with fitted wardrobes.

I notice as Chaos is putting clothes from his bag into draws in the dresser and some in a wash basket in the corner, he is moving slowly and as if he is in pain.

"I'll sleep on the sofa or in with one of the other if that would make you feel more comfortable."

Watching him a little longer, I have to ask.

CHAOS

"Chaos are you in pain?" I ask softly as I take a seat on the end of the bed, bag still in hand.

He stops what he's doing and turns to look at me.

"What makes you think I'm in pain"

Really? I can see it written all over his face and in the way he moves. Giving him a look, he smiles.

"I'm not as young as I was once and due to a few accidents, my muscles don't handle long rides like they used to. I'll be fine after a soak in the bath."

NINE

CHAOS

MY muscles are killing me but no way am I admitting that to her. No way.

I'm not weak man by any means but I am human and I'm not getting any younger. Being in my mid-thirties now and having a few minor bike accidents under my belt, the beating my muscles take from a long run is getting worse. I can feel the ache in my shoulders and my back. Plus, my legs are not missing out on the pain either. Jesus Christ, if this my thirties, I'm not sure I'll make it forty. Trying to not show the pain, I carry on moving some of my things to other draws to make room for Olivia and her things.

Poor girl only has one fucking bag. If she's going to stay here with us, were going to need to get her some more clothes and shoes. She has biker boots on at the minute but sneaking a look, she could do with new ones, they seem worn. It makes me angry that she has so little and yet she was with her dad, who should have been doing his job and providing properly for her. Not having worn boots or being treated as if she's the fucking maid. The rage I felt at her being mistreated like that by people, who should be having her back and treating her like family is engulfing. I push it down though as I don't want to scare her again. I never want to scare her, ever. I feel a small hand on my shoulder and turn to look at her.

"I can help you with the pain," she offers.

She must read something on my face but she quickly steps away.

"Not like that. I mean I trained as a masseuse when I first left school. If you have any massage oils, Tiger balm or even some body moisturisers, I help your muscles."

Oh. My. God, if she could take my pain away.

"I know you didn't mean it that way and I would never expect that of you Sweetpea. I told you, you are safe here and will be treated with respect," I try to reassure her.

Thinking, I'm sure one of the brothers got me a massage kit as a joke one Christmas, I walk into the bathroom, hunt around at the back of the cupboard, and find the stupid giftset. Coming back into the bedroom, I hand it to Liv and shrug my shoulders.

"One of the brothers gave it to me as a joke one Christmas. Funny fuckers. Been in the back of the cupboard a few years, so not sure how much use it will be."

She gives me a soft smile and I feel my heart skip a beat. I want her to smile like that all the time.

"It will work fine; it just helps my hands move easier on your skin and relax the muscles. Can you change into shorts or something that gives me access to your back and legs please?" she asks as she leaves the room.

I find a pair of old loose basketball shorts and quickly change into them. I'm sitting on the bed when Liv comes back with some towels from the bathroom. She lays them on the bed from the bottom to the top up the middle.

"Can you lay on the towels please with your head at the bottom of the bed and lay on your front?" she asks.

Doing as I'm told; I lay on the towels on my front and get comfy. Liv stands at the bottom of the bed with my head practically between her legs.

Oh God. I am really glad I'm laid on my front and she can't see my cock growing hard.

When she leans over and her core is closer, and I bite my lip to stop the groan that is stuck in my throat.

This is going to be torture.

I feel the warm oil hit between my shoulder blades and her hands start to spread it across the top of my back, up to my shoulders and along them. Once she has spread it all, she starts to work the muscles with her fingers. The groan that was stuck in my throat slips free and my whole body relaxes.

"Just relax and concentrate on your breathing," she says.

Doing as I'm told; I feel my body start to relax more as her nimble hands work the muscles in my back. She's working her way from my shoulders and neck, down to the bottom of my back. All while my head is still between her thighs. This feels amazing, like angels are dancing on my back. It only feels like minutes but is probably longer when I lose the feeling of her hands on me and I let out an unhappy grumble. Her tinkle of a giggle reaches my ears, and hear the cap of the oil and then the bed drips near my legs. Her hands are now working my leg muscles.

I need to marry this woman.

Her hands are gliding up and down my thighs, working the tight muscles. Once she's finished with my calves, she starts on my feet.

Who knew having a woman's hands on you in a non-sexual like this, could feel almost as good as sex. I said almost.

"Jesus, Sweetpea this feels," I tell her as she finishes with my feet and starts back gently sweeping my muscles on my back, then my neck.

Then slowly moving her hands into my hair as she crouches in front of me and massages my head. I'm pretty sure I couldn't speak right now even if I tried.

"There all done. Does that feel better?" she asks

I struggle for a few minutes to get myself together so I can form an actual sentence and not embarrass myself.

"Jesus Liv. Sweetpea that was pure heaven. You've got fucking magic hands, I feel like a new man."

There's that giggle again.

"Glad I could help. You go take a hot shower now to relax the muscles further and also wash the oil off," she orders as she leaves the bedroom.

I remain laying on the bed a few moments, willing my cock to behave enough where I can get off the bed and not make a fool of myself. Giving up, as no way is he going down anytime soon, I get off the bed and gather the towels off the bed. Using them like a shield, I head for the bedroom.

"I cleared out the top two drawers in the dresser for you. If you need hanging space let me know," I tell her and rush into the bathroom.

Turning the shower on, I wait for it to get hot and step under the stream. Lowering my head, I let the water run over me.

Unable to help myself, I take my cock in hand just needing to feel some relief. I imagine my head back between Liv's thighs, but this time she's naked. I run my hands up and down her legs, slowly kissing my way to her centre. My tongue darts out and licks her from bottom to top. I growl as I imagine how sweet she tastes. I wonder what the little noises she makes as I take her clit in between my teeth and nibble. A tingle runs up my spine and that's all it takes; I shoot my load all over the shower with Liv's name falling from my lips.

Jesus, that is hardest I've come in a long time.

Quickly washing up and cleaning the shower wall, I dry and slip my shorts back on. In my rush I forgot to grab clean clothes. Slipping out the bathroom, I notice Liv is in the kitchen, so I rush to the bedroom and dress. Meeting her back in the living area, I ask if she's unpacked.

"Yeah, I only packed enough for the weekend at the rally, so I didn't have a lot to unpack," she replies shyly.

Yeah, that's not going to wash with me.

"Babes, if you need more clothes, we can either buy you some or get your dad to send you some."

"Oh no, I'm okay. I can just wash what I have and make do."

CHAOS

The look on her face tells me she's hiding something and I have an awful feeling what it might be.

"Liv, you do have other clothes at home, right?"

Her face goes bright red and looks down so she doesn't meet my eyes.

Fuck, I knew it.

"Yeah, of course," she replies while still not looking up.

"You wouldn't be lying to me now, would you?"

Her head shoots up.

"No Chaos. I honestly have some more clothes at home."

"But?" I know there is a *but*.

"They are a little worn and old," she says as she covers her face with her hands.

She looks so embarrassed. Her dad should be ashamed of himself, letting her live like this. She deserves to be treasured and worshipped. Walking over to her, I slowly lower her hands and take her into my arms for a hug. I notice how perfect she fits as I wrap my arms around her and rest my head on top of hers.

"Everything will be okay from on Sweetpea. We are going to get you some new clothes and anything else you may need. Do not argue with me on this, otherwise I will just check the size of your current stuff and order for you. Trust me, you do not want that," I end on a chuckle.

I feel her chuckle in my chest and call me a stubborn bossy caveman. This makes my chuckle more.

"Come on, let's see what the others are up to."

I lead her out the room and back down to the common room. Mayhem and Riot are chilling on the sofas with a drink. Psycho is at the bar, sat on the stool in the corner, watching the room. The rest of the brothers are dotted about the place. Heading to the bar, I grab us both a beer from the prospect and head for the sofa.

"Pres," Mayhem nods and smile at Liv.

"You settle in, okay?" he asks her

She just nods her head and takes a drink of her beer.

"Erm Pres, you seem to have spring in your step. How come? I can barely move off this sofa," Riot moans.

Smirking at his complaining, I tell them about Liv's magic hands and Riot perks up at this.

"Liv, can you do me?" he asks with his fucking grin.

The man is gay but still can't help flirting with the ladies. Jesus he is a handful at times.

Liv looks to me as if to ask it's okay. I like that but I also want her to feel comfortable enough to be who she is.

"Up to you Sweetpea," I tell her.

She smiles and disappears back to the room, coming back a few minutes later with a towel and the oil and pulls a chair over and places it next to the sofa.

"Can you sit in the chair and remove your shirt please Riot?"

He does as she says and she puts some oil in hands, rubbing them together. Once Riot is in place, she starts to massage his shoulders and neck. The fucker is making all sorts of sex noises, moaning, and groaning. I can see Liv getting redder and redder so I kick his leg to stop.

"Pack it in with the fucking noises," I growl.

"Can't help it boss. You were right, she has magic hands."

Liv smiles at this and notices the rest of the brothers

CHAOS

are lining up.

Fuckers.

Once she's finished with Riot, Mayhem is next and then even Psycho gets in on the action.

"She's a keeper," Psycho whispers as he walks past me, slapping me on the shoulder and I nod in understanding.

He's right, she is. Liv has fitted perfectly into club and she's only been here a few hours. I notice she's now looking a little tired. It was a long ride for her too, so I grab my laptop from the office and then lead her back to my room. The brothers call goodnight out to her and she waves back. I can't help the smile on my face. Getting comfy on the sofa, I log her into the laptop and hand her my bank card.

"Order what ya need babes and don't just order a little either. I mean kit yourself out. If I don't think you've ordered enough, I will order more. I need to catch up on some bits in the office. If you need me, I'll be there but I won't be long," I tell her as I leave her to get sorted.

Heading back down, I nod at Mayhem, Riot and Psycho to join me and we all head for my office.

"Well, it has been an interesting weekend, that's for sure," Riot says as he takes a seat on the sofa I have in my office.

"Fucked up is what it is," Mayhem says, flopping down in chair next to my desk.

"Clusterfuck," Psycho says.

Man of few words.

"I like Liv, she feels like a little sister," Riot says and Mayhem nods.

I love the brothers have taken to her like this, it means I've got more chance of her staying. I take out my phone and ring Judge.

"Judge."

"It's Chaos. Thought you would want to know Liv made it back safe and is okay."

There is silence and then he lets out a breath.

"Thank fuck."

"You need to start explaining more Judge," I warn

"I know and thank you for not pushing it at the rally. I love my daughter but recently I've not been the man she deserves and I'm letting her down. Dyno wants her and my club. I'm pretty sure he is behind Voodoo's disappearance."

I look at Mayhem and Psycho who both nod.

"I'll get Keys and Tracker onto it. See what they can find."

"Thank you, Chaos. Voodoo wouldn't leave his sister like that; they are really close. Dyno is not going to take this well. He's already muttering about taking her back"

Riot jumps up at that but I hold my hand up to stop him, even Mayhem and Psycho look pissed. Clearly, she's made an impact on all of us.

"She is safe here and we will look after her. The brothers are fond of her already."

"My girl ain't no whore," Judge shouts.

"Calm yourself Judge, that is not what I meant," I warn.

"The brothers see her more like a little sister. However, my feels are not of a brother sister type, but we will leave that for now," I tell him straight up.

"If Liv feels the same way, then I'll not stand in your way Chaos. Your dad was good and honourable man, I have feeling you are the same way. As long as you treat her right and better than she has been treated recently, then we have no problems."

"Let me know if Dyno makes any moves."

Ending the call, I tell them we will discuss it further in church. Mayhem says he will speak with Keys and Tracker tonight.

"I'll you all in the morning," I say as we leave my office, and head back to my room.

Entering, I find Liv curled up asleep on the sofa. She looks so cute all curled up. At some point she has changed into sleep shorts and a tank top.

Fuck I want to run my hands over her curves.

Being the gentleman I am, I go into the bedroom and turn the bedding down. Grabbing the basketball shorts from earlier, I head back into the living room. Scooping Liv up off the sofa, she snuggles into my chest, my name falling from her lips.

"I got you Sweetpea," I say as I kiss her head.

Carrying her to bed, I gently place on the bed and tuck her in. She gets comfy and falls straight back to sleep. I grab a pillow and spare sheet from the cupboard, heading for a uncomfortable night on the sofa.

amazing

TEN

OLIVIA

WAKING, I can feel the sun on my face. I've been here at the clubhouse now a few days and have to admit it is a totally different feel to my dad's clubhouse. All the brothers have been so welcoming and kind. No one has ordered me around or forced me into doing anything I didn't want to do. However, in the last few days I have cleaned the clubhouse and cooked for everyone, let's face it, they are men and have no clue really about housework or cooking.

I try to move on the bed but I seemed to be pend in by two rather large objects. Smiling, I know exactly what those objects are, my new shadows. Neither King or Raze lets me out of their sight for long and love to sleep on the bed with me. I slowly get out of bed and head to the bathroom to start my morning routine. I can see Chaos laid out on the sofa; his feet are sticking out the end.

Aww, I feel bad that he has given up his bed for me. He

really does not look comfy. He starts move and I dart into the bathroom. Going about my morning business, I try to be as quiet as possible. Sneaking back into kitchen, I fill the kettle and start quietly opening cupboards to make myself a morning tea.

"One going for me?" a gravelly voice calls behind me, making me scream and spin round.

"Shit, sorry Liv," Chaos says with a guilty look.

Within moments of my scream the dogs come running from the bedroom barking and growling, putting themselves between Chaos and me. I take a few seconds to steady myself.

"God, you scared me. Don't sneak up on me like that," I scold him while stroking Raze and King's heads to let them know I'm okay.

A cheeky smile crosses his lips.

"Was kind of funny."

"To you," I smirk back.

He walks into the kitchen and nudges me out of the way.

"I'll make the drinks, what do you like?" he asks moving around from the cupboard to the drawer.

"Tea, milk with one sugar please," I say as I head for the sofa and start folding the covers and place them along with the pillow on the chair.

"Thanks, Sweetpea," he says as he joins me on the sofa once the tea is ready.

I take the cup in both hands and breath in the delicious scent. Just taking a few moments before I have that first sip.

"Mmm, you make good tea," I tell him, turning to face

him.

I blush at the look of desire and lust on his face, his eyes twinkle, making me squirm in my seat.

"Did you get everything you needed the other day ordered?" he asks on a cough.

I dip my head and take a sip of my drink before I answer him.

"Yeah, I ordered what I would need. I didn't want to spend too much, I will pay you back," I promise.

He shakes his head and flicks the TV on and we sit in silence drinking our tea while watching breakfast TV.

"Hungry?" Chaos asks me a little a later.

"I could eat."

Nodding, he places my hands in his and leads me downstairs to where the brothers are starting to gather, ready to start their day. As I'm walking towards what I assume is the kitchen, I feel a small body hit smack into my legs with an oomph. Looking down I notice a cute little boy sitting on the floor.

"Oh, sweetheart are you okay?"

"You pwetty," he replies.

Chuckling, I crouch down in front of him.

"Thank you, you're very handsome too."

A groan comes from behind me.

"Mayhem, your kid is a little flirt," Chaos shouts

"I'm Logan and I is four," the little man tells me while he stands up and holds out his hand.

Grinning, I take his hand to shake it, the little man lifts my hand, kissing it. Another groan from Chaos has Logan smiling.

"Mayhem," he bellows again.

"Way too much like his dad," Riot mutters as he walks past with a wink.

"Way too much like his uncles," I counter, getting another wink and a laugh from Riot.

Turning back to Logan, I can see him trying to wink but he's just blinking. It really is the sweetest thing ever.

"Come on Romeo, let's find your dad," Chaos says as he sweeps Logan into his arms.

Shit, I think my ovaries just exploded. There is something so sexy about a man with a child in their arms.

Heading into the kitchen, we notice Mayhem fixing some toast with chocolate spread.

"You causing havoc Logan?" Mayhem asks without turning round.

"I'm a good boy," Logan replies, trying to wink again.

Jesus this kid is priceless.

Shaking his head, Chaos sits Logan at a table.

"Kid is hitting on Liv already, kissing her hand, trying to wink, which I have to admit was fucking funny, even called her pretty."

'That's my boy," Mayhem laughs.

He places the plate of toast in front of Logan and wraps a towel round his front. I sit at the table with him, watching him get more chocolate round his mouth than in it. I can't help but smile watching the little guy. Mayhem keeps checking on him every so often as he talks to Chaos in the kitchen area. He really is a good dad. A plate of buttery toasts is placed in front of me and I tuck in with

Logan.

"You manage to actually get any chocolate in your mouth?" Mayhem asks, walking up with a wipe.

Logan just grins and oh lord those dimples, he is going to be trouble when he's older.

"Come on Lo, time to head for Nanny and Pops," Mayhem says as Logan jumps down from his seat.

"Bye Liv," he waves.

"Bye sweetheart, have fun," I call back.

I watch his little butt waddle away, holding Mayhem's hand and my ovaries are exploding again. I'm not going to last with all these men showing a softer side. My hormones can't cope with it all.

"You okay Sweetpea?" Chaos asks as he gently strokes my arm.

Now this man has the power to destroy me if I let him. Nodding, I go back to eating my toast as King and Raze snore at my feet.

"Fancy taking the boys for a walk? We have a lovely walk close by through some woods that lead to pond. Fuck do these two-love water," Chaos laughs.

"Yeah, that would actually be really nice."

Nodding, he clears my plate away and we head outside. Grabbing two leads and a checked shirt, he hands me the shirt.

"You might get a little cold on the walk and I notice you didn't have a light coat or anything. Just tie it round your waist for now babes."

Doing as I'm told; I tie it round my waist as we walk

towards an old land rover, painted the usual army green and beaten up. The dogs hop in the back and get comfy and notice towels and bottled water are already in the back. Chaos opens the passenger side for me.

"Such a gentleman," I say getting in.

"Welcome my lady," he replies with a bow.

He really isn't what you would expect when you first meet him. Chaos has a bit of a soft playful side that he keeps hidden from people who aren't in his inner circle. It means a lot to me that he feels comfortable with me enough to show me that side of his personality. It's not long before we are pulling up to a wooded area and parking up and the boys in the back are getting excited. Guess they have been before so know what's coming.

"Sit," Chaos tells them and they both instantly do at the command.

Getting them both on a lead, he hands me Raze.

"He's a little easier on the lead then King."

I smile that he has thought about my safety. He locks the car and we head off into the woods with the dogs walking at our sides. It really is a beautiful walk; the woods are thick with wild flowers growing around them and the birds singing in the trees. We are not walking long before our hands catch

"Sorry," he mumbles.

It happens a few times more as we walk along just enjoying the peace. When it happens again, Chaos keeps a hold of my hand and laces his fingers through mine. Our hands fit perfectly together. A tingle runs through me, no one has ever made me feel the way Chaos does. The past few days he has taken every chance he could to innocently touch me but touch me none the less. A hand on my shoulder, the small of my back, my thigh or calf while curled up on the sofa watching TV. Just some part of us touching, connecting in a way. It all just feels easy, relaxed and right with him and the rest of the brothers.

"We're having a BBQ this weekend to welcome you and so you can meet everyone. You'll even get to meet Mayhem's folks. Babs and Leon are amazing people, Benny boy might even come too, he's Mayhem's brother." Chaos tells me.

Okay, this has thrown me a little.

"Why are you having a welcome BBQ? I am only here until my dad gets the rest of the money; he owes you."

I am totally confused now. I know we were getting a little close but surely, he doesn't want me to stay.

"Liv, I know that is how you originally came to be here with us but that was not the first time you caught my eye. I saw you a few times round the stalls at the rally and I couldn't stop looking for you. Your beauty drew me in, I'm hoping even after your dad finds the rest of the money and things are safe back home for you, that you will consider staying. I'm going to be honest with you and I hope you will be honest with me too?"

"I will always be honest with you," I promise.

We've come to a clearing with a wide-open field and some benches around the edge, with large pond off to the side. We take a seat on a bench close to the water, letting the dogs off the lead. The pair of them take one look at us and then dart straight into the water with a splash.

Chaos turns me so I'm facing him and takes my hands in his.

"I'm going to lay it all out there for you. I feel a connection with you Liv. Something I have not felt before. Sitting here with you, your hand in mine, sitting on the sofa watching TV, it just feels so comfortable and right. I panic when I don't know where you are or can't see you in the common room. Every time I see you, I want to take you in my arms and kiss you. I want to build on this and see where we can take it us. I want you to stay, with me."

ELEVEN

CHAOS

I'VE just laid it all out for her and I am praying she doesn't shout me down. Everything I've said to her is true and from the heart. She makes me feel things no one else ever has but also, she makes me feel comfortable enough to show her the true me. Show her all the sides of me as I know she won't judge or think less of me.

Liv is the type of honest, down to earth girl who doesn't judge anyone and accepts people for who they are. She is so kind and caring. *Fuck*, watching her with Lo today caused a ache in my chest. It felt like I had been missing something from my life before and now I realise it was her. I want to build a life and family with her. I've never thought about being a dad before, not even when Mayhem had Lo. I love being that little shits uncle but it didn't make me want kids of my own. Olivia on the other hand, has been in my life a mere few days and has been wanting things I've never wanted before.

CHAOS

Taking her face in my hands, I look into her eyes, searching for something. Hope maybe, a sign she wants this too.

After a few seconds, she leans in and that my sign. My lips crash onto hers as my tongue sweeps around her lips, begging to be let in, just for a taste and she doesn't disappoint.

This kiss is fireworks, I feel myself tingle and grow harder than ever before. She tastes amazing and I growl into the kiss as I move one hand to the back of head to pull her closer, as the other slides down her back. I'm so lost in the most heavenly kiss I have ever had, and forget where we are until suddenly a large wet beast jumps on.

"Raze," I command and Liv squeals as both dog's shake covering us head to toe in water, killing the moment.

Both of us sit there covered in water as the dogs run off again, silently we turn to look at each other and burst out laughing.

"That was hilarious," she giggles.

"You best be talking about the dogs, otherwise you might dent my ego," I laugh.

"Your ego is just fine," she sasses back and my cock starts to get hard again.

I stroke her hair back from her face and lean forward for another quick kiss.

"Best kiss of my life," I tell her.

"Was pretty good," she says with a cheeky smile.

"Now my ego definitely just took a hit. Pretty good is not good enough."

Laughing, the little minx skips away from me and after

the dogs.

"You'll have to try harder next time," she taunts.

"Oh, I'll show you harder."

I take off running after her, picking her up and twirling her around. Her laugh is the most beautiful sound I have ever heard. Pulling her into my arms, I kiss her hard, pouring everything into the kiss.

"Better?"

"Oh yeah, you're getting the hang of it," she says with dazed look on her face.

"Guess I need more practise then."

Cupping her hand in mine, we walk back to the dogs and put them on the lead, then head back for the car and clubhouse. After the dogs showered us with mucky pond water, we both need shower.

Fuck, I'm hard again thinking about Liv in the shower.

Once we are back at the clubhouse, I hand the dogs over to the prospects.

"Use plenty of dog shampoo on them, they've been in disgusting pond water. Fuck only knows what's floating in it."

I feel Liv shiver next me and give her a confused look.

"That disgusting pond water is all over us Chaos, we need showers quick."

The look on her face is hilarious. I grab her hand again and lead her to my room and straight into the bathroom. Closing us both inside, I start the shower to warm up and begin to remove my clothes. I have my shirt off and I'm unbuttoning my jeans when I notice Liv hasn't moved.

"The idea of a shower Liv is you get in with no clothes on."

This gets me an eye roll.

Jesus her sass is coming out the more comfortable she gets and I for one love it.

"Yeah, I think by now in life I know how to get a shower Chaos."

"Declan."

"Huh?"

"Declan, my name is Declan."

"Okay, nice name but what does that have to do with the fact I am not getting a shower with you?"

Oh, we are so playing now.

"When we alone or to be honest just around my brothers you can call me Declan, but not around other clubs or other chapters."

"I know the rules," she says with another eye roll.

"Good, second, yes you are showering with me. Thought we were giving this a go between us?"

I'm gifted another eye roll, how she doesn't have headache from these she's giving out is beyond me.

"Love a good eye roll, don't you?"

Her cheeks instantly blush.

"I'm sorry, I don't always know I'm doing them. I had to try really hard to be more aware recently but I guess that's slipped a little."

I'm instantly pissed and stalk towards her, caging her in against the bathroom door. My arms go either side of her head and I lower mine, so our noses are nearly touching.

"Don't you ever hide how you feel from me or any of

my brothers. I love your sass and it makes me feel ten feet tall that you feel confident and safe enough around us to be your true self. No one will ever cause harm to you ever again."

I finish with a kiss; her luscious lips are soft and she tastes amazing. My hands slide down and grips the hem of her t-shirt, lifting it up, only breaking the kiss to pull it over her head. Then I am back kissing her, my hands find her waist as I caress the soft skin at the top of her jeans, untying the shirt, letting it fall to floor. Her hands find my jeans as we quickly finish undressing each other, all while still kissing. It's more than kissing now, as we seem to be devouring each other, our hands are everywhere.

"Legs up baby," I quickly say as I cup her arse and lift her into me.

Her legs go round my waist and arms round my neck. Once I have her in my arms, I walk us into the shower, letting the water run over us.

"Okay no more. I really want this gross pond water off me please," she says breaking the kiss and lowering her legs.

"Wash quickly," I growl.

With the speed of light, we finish the showering, dry and head for the bedroom. Liv leaps onto the bed and lays waiting for me.

"Fuck you are beautiful," I tell her as I grab her ankle and pull her to the end of the bed. "I need a taste of this pretty pussy."

Her breath hitches as I kneel on the floor between her open legs and kiss my way to her centre. One lick and I'm gone. She tastes like heaven. A breathy moan escapes from her and that's my cue, I go town on her like I'm a starved man and this is my last meal. It's not long before she is arching under me and calling my name as her orgasm ripples through her. Giving her one more kiss on the swollen lips, I crawl between her legs until I'm hovering over her and kiss her so she can taste how amazing she is. I feel her hand slide down my chest between us and grip my cock as she guides me to her entrance.

"I need you," she pants.

"What the lady wants, she gets."

I slowly push inside her warm heat and I swear my eyes cross with the pleasure of being inside her. She eclipses every other woman I have ever been with. I hold still until I feel her start to wiggle. That pushes me over the edge and I start to pound away, losing all rhythm with how fucking perfect she feels around me.

"Holy shit, Declan," she screams as I feel another orgasm go through her, and a few thrusts later I join her over the edge.

The tingle up my spine is so intense I forget how to breath for a second and I come harder than I thought possible.

I fall to the side unable to keep myself up and pull her into me, wrapping my arms around her, while we both fight to get our breaths back. Her arms come around me and her breath tickles my chest as we both fall asleep, wrapped in each other.

TWELVE

OLIVIA

I wake feeling too hot and something heavy around my waist, and also feel something poking me in my back. Giggling to myself, I remember the most amazing sex of my life. Chaos really knows what he is doing. I slowly lift his arm off me so I can slip out of bed.

I freeze when he murmurs in sleep and rolls onto his back, taking the cover with him, so it is just covering him from the waist down. Silently as possible, I head for the bathroom to do my business. Coming back into the bedroom, I stop in the doorway, watching this perfect man sleep. He looks so peaceful laid there. His chest has a few tattoos and chiselled abs. He looks almost super human, like he isn't real. I can feel myself falling more and more for him. He must have a flaw, something as no one is that perfect.

He suddenly lets out the loudest, biggest snore, making not only myself jump but startling himself a little, causing him to roll onto his front and then a loud fart erupts from his pert sexy behind.

Yup, there's the flaw, he's a man.

I can't help the giggle, and put my hand over my mouth to try to muffle the sound but I totally lose it when he farts again. I am clinging to the doorway with tears rolling down my face, just unable to catch my breath from laughing so much, which in turn wakes him up.

"You okay babes? What's so funny?"

He looks so confused and I don't have the heart to tell him but I'm now doubled over with my hands on my knees, just in hysterics. The main door opens slightly and both dogs come belting through, nearly taking me out as they rush past me to dive on the bed. This doesn't help me to stop laughing and now I need the bathroom again. Once I've managed to calm myself down, I head back to the bedroom and notice that Chaos is still laid in bed, propped up on the pillows waiting for me.

"You over your giggles?"

I chuckle and slide in next to him.

"Yeah," I sigh.

His arm comes around me and pulls me into him. Resting my head on his chest, my arm rests across his stomach and lay in silence, just enjoying each other. The buzz of his mobile disrupts our peace.

"Chaos."

I can't hear what the other person is saying but from Chaos' face, it isn't good.

"Be there in a moment," he finishes the call and quickly sends a text.

"Liv, I don't want you panic but Dyno is at the gate."

Okay, he can say don't panic all he likes but I'm going to fucking panic. Of course, I'm going to panic.

"I won't let him get you, I promise. Just stay here."

Oh hell no.

"Erm, I don't think so. If you promise he won't get me then I need to show I'm not hiding and stand with you."

I know how this works; we need show him a united front. Chaos nods, like he understands my thinking.

"You stay next to me and close to Riot at all times."

Nodding, we quickly get dressed and head downstairs. At the last second, I call for the boys and they leap from their beds and walk either side of me. Chaos gives me a questioning look.

"Dyno is scared of dogs," I say with grin.

As we head outside, Riot appears at my side, Mayhem is at Chaos' side and Psycho is already at the gate, leaning against the post, playing with his knife like he's bored.

As we get to the gate I can see Dyno, he has Rattle and Lizard with him.

"Chaos, I have the rest of your money, Olivia, go get your things," he orders, like he's in charge.

No one moves. The dogs are siting either side of me, eyes trained on Dyno. I place a hand on each of their heads and stroke. This makes Dyno look down and he notices them, and I can instantly see the fear in his eyes.

"Now Olivia," he shouts at me, causing King and Raze to stand, growling their displeasure.

Dyno takes a step back and Chaos puts his arm around

my shoulders and whispers

"Good idea with the dogs babes," he kisses the side of my head and I lean into him.

Seeing this, Dyno's eyes get hard with anger.

"Psycho, get the cash from him."

Psycho slowly stands from the post and nonchalantly walks to the gate, holding out his hand for the money to passed through. He hands it off to Dolla, who I didn't see appear. Twisted, the prospect is still in the gatehouse, watching with his gun drawn ready.

"Dolla?" Chaos questions.

"All twenty thousand is there."

"Perfect, that our business done. I'll make sure to speak with Judge, thanks for bringing the cash." Chaos says as he turns us and we start back towards the clubhouse.

"Chaos, you still have something of mine," Dyno shouts.

We stop and Chaos looks over his shoulder.

"I have nothing of yours."

We carry on walking; I can hear a scuffle behind me but I don't look back.

"She is mine Chaos and I will have her back. Mark my words, you can't keep her behind these gates forever. She's mine.'

I shudder as Dyno is losing his mind behind us.

"Keep walking, don't look back baby," Chaos kisses my head again.

I know I need to trust him but Jesus, when is Dyno going to get the message? I really have had enough of him and want my life back; I want to live free.

Back inside the clubhouse, Chaos leads me into his office and I flop down onto the sofa. Mayhem, Riot and Psycho have joined us.

"Don't worry Liv, he won't get you. He'll have to get through me first," Riot says trying to comfort me, pulling me into a hug.

"He'll have to get through us all," Mayhem confirms.

Psycho just nods.

"Thanks guys. It means a lot you have my back."

Chaos smiles at me, picking up his phone. I know he's calling my dad.

"Chaos, everything okay?"

"Yeah Judge, we got your payment."

Silence.

"Erm, what payment?"

"Judge, we just had a visit from Dyno and a few of your men. He paid the remaining balance."

More silence

"Chaos, I would check that money, it hasn't come from me or the club."

Psycho disappears out the door, returning a few moments later with Dolla.

"Check the money."

Nodding, Dolla puts the money on a table and starts checking it all over. Declan hands him a light from the draw in the desk, which Dolla uses to check all the notes.

"All present and correct. Its legit," he tells us.

"Put it straight in the safe," Chaos tells him and Dolla leaves the room with the money.

"You hear that Judge. All legal tender and in full."

"Where the fuck has that sneaky bastard got that much money from? He's not been at the clubhouse for a few days."

"That's for you to find out."

"Yeah, I'm working on it, but shit is not good here."

"If you need help, let me know. I'll see what Keys has managed to find."

"Thanks, keep me posted. How's Olivia?"

Chaos gives me a look and I smile back but keep quiet.

"She's good, making her my Ol' lady."

I can't hide the shock from my face. I know we agreed to try and see where the this took us but Jesus' fuck. Making me his Ol' lady is a big deal and one we have not talked about yet.

"You best take care of her and make her happy, but Chaos, if this is not something she wants, then I will be there as fast as I can to bring her home."

"She is home Judge. I would give my life to make her happy."

The sincerity on his face makes my heart sing.

"That's all a father wants to hear. Keep me informed."

Ending the call without another word, Chaos stands from the desk.

"Welcome to the family Liv," Riot says as he kisses me on the head.

Everyone leaves except for me and Chaos.

"You going to give me chance and be my Ol' lady Liv?"

Seriously, he wants this?

"Declan, that is a big step. We've only just agreed to give us a try. What happens if you realise, we are not suited?"

He comes around the desk and scoops me into his arms. "I know you're my future."

His soft lips touch mine and the second I kiss him back, he cups my head, deepening the kiss, pouring everything he has into the kiss, showing me what he wants and feels.

"Okay Declan, I'll be your Ol' lady."

THIRTEEN

CHAOS

I can't believe she has agreed to be my Ol' lady. I really thought she would've put up more of a fight but I'm glad she didn't. If she, had I would have fought for her and shown her I'm serious. That woman is everything to me and I know it's fast but sometimes you have to follow your gut. My gut is telling me two things right now. One, that Olivia is it for me. Two, all is not well with Tribal Bones, plus I fear it is only going to get worse before it gets better.

Kissing Olivia again, I love the dazed expression on her face.

"Babe, I need to get to church but why don't you go chill with the dogs."

"Okay honey, I'll be in our room."

Jesus, her calling me honey and saying our room does something to me.

"Love you calling me honey."

Smacking her arse as she walks past me, she heads up

the stairs and I head to church. Time to get this shit resolved so Liv can have peace. As my queen she deserves that. I'm the last one to arrive in church and take my place at the head of the table.

"Keys, I need you on Tribal Bones. I want to know everything on the wanker crew as Liv so kindly calls them."

Keys nods and starts typing away on his laptop. It is never far from him.

"I spoke to Judge and he has no idea where the money Dyno just paid us came from, but it definitely was not Judge or the club. He confirmed he has no idea that Dyno or his boys were even here. They've not been at the clubhouse for a few days."

"Got a bad feeling about this," Psycho says.

"You and me both," Mayhem seconds.

"I agree. Judge did say that shit was not good at the moment. From previous conversations and watching how Dyno behaved, I wouldn't put it passed him to try to take Judge out."

"I'll reach out to Archer to see what I can find out and if they need help," Riot offers.

"Good idea. We need to be on our toes. Okay, we can't do more until Keys does his thing. Once we have more information, we will have church again to put a plan in place, Olivia deserves peace."

There's nodding all round from the boys.

"Speaking of Olivia, she has agreed to be my Ol' lady. Anyone have a problem with that?"

All's quiet, no one says a word but they all have shit

eating grins on their faces.

"No one got anything to say?"

"Nope Prez, I like Liv, she's good for you," Riot says.

Psycho nods his agreement

"She fits in, she's kind and welcoming to everyone," Tracker adds.

"She's brilliant with Lo, plus she understands this life" Mayhem likes anyone who is good with Lo.

"She just accepts us as we are," Dolla adds.

"Liv is even nice to the prospects; she doesn't talk down to them," Psycho finally adds.

"Okay, Olivia is now your first lady. Dolla, I want a cut ordering for her, Sweetpea as her name."

"Congrats Pres," Dolla says which sets them all off cheering and banging the table.

"Alright settle down. That is all for now, we have the family BBQ in two weeks' time, so be present for that. Keys, I need an update as soon as possible."

I slam the gavel down ending church, and the brothers all file out, leaving me in peace.

Dyno is definitely not going to go easy; I feel it in my bones that shit is only going to get worse. The look that he was giving Olivia; he is not going to give up without a fight. That fucker will fight dirty and hard. Men like that don't like to be told no, they like things their way and their way only. Well, he's got another thing coming if he thinks I'm going to roll over and give up Olivia. He made her life a misery before and I am so angry at Judge for letting it happen.

If I had a daughter, I would protect her with my life.

Thinking of children has me wondering what Olivia would look like all round, growing our child.

Fuck, why does that image make me hard?

I hope she wants children; I haven't really considered it before but now? Yeah, now I want children. I didn't think of them before because I never considered I would find a woman who would put up with me, my brothers, and our lifestyle. Olivia really is a one in a million and she's mine.

"You okay in here?" Mayhem asks, sticking his head round the door.

"Yeah, just thinking."

"Where is Liv," he asks, joining me back at the table.

"Upstairs with the dogs. I can't believe I've lost my dogs to her, they follow her around, sleep on her side of the bed and are really protective of her."

"It's a good thing," he chuckles.

"Added security for her."

"So, what had you thinking so hard in here on your own?"

"Just going over shit in my head. I've a really bad feeling shit is going to get worse before it gets any better. I wouldn't put anything passed Dyno."

"I agree Chaos. I think we need to warn Judge."

I think on that a moment, it wouldn't hurt, I don't think.

"You're right, it wouldn't hurt."

I pull out my phone and dial Judge.

"Judge."

"It's Chaos. We've been talking and think you need to be extra careful. I wouldn't put it passed Dyno to try and take you out."

All's quiet for a few on the other end

"Judge?"

"Yeah, sorry Chaos, I'm here. You're not wrong and thanks for giving me a heads up. I wouldn't put it passed him either."

Mayhem and me exchange a look. Judge's voice doesn't sound right.

"You okay man?"

"I'll be honest with you, no I'm not. Shit is not good here. Dyno is challenging me and the brothers have started choosing sides already. Facing off on each other, whole club is a fucking mess."

Okay, now that is worrying.

"Anything we can do to help. Already got Keys looking into Dyno and his wanker crew."

"Wanker crew," he laughs.

"Courtesy of Liv, that one."

"My girl is a spitfire for sure. Just keep her safe Chaos."

"Will do and let me know if you need anything. I'll be back in touch when I have something."

"I appreciate it."

Ending the call, I look to Mayhem.

"Well, that didn't fucking sound good," he tells me.

"Not at all brother. Let's see what Keys finds out, hopefully it won't be too long."

"He's good at what he does. Now fuck off and see your woman."

Laughing, I leave church and head upstairs to find my dog thief.

It's been two weeks since all the drama with Dyno. He's been way too quiet which is starting to make me itch. My gut is screaming at me that all is not well and shit is about to go down. The unrest and nervous energy around the club the last few days has made the brothers on edge.

Deciding I'm going to make sure all is as it should be, I decide to check in with Keys. He's been working night and day to find as much information as he can about Dyno and his wanker crew. Knocking on his door, it takes a few minutes before he shouts to come in.

"Prez, what can I do you for?" he asks without turning away from his computers.

"Err, how did you know it was me?"

He points to a screen at the side which shows him all the camera's around the compound, including one in the hall, you can clearly see his door.

"Smart fucker," I grumble.

He just nods and keeps typing.

"Wondered how you were getting on?"

He stops and finally turns to look at me. Fuck he looks tired and in need of a good shower. Once he gets deep into something, he tends to forget important things such as personal care, sleep, and food. I make a note to myself to make sure the prospects bring him regular meals and to check on him more often.

"It's not good Prez. Dyno has been making deals behind the clubs back and not sharing the wealth. He's got bank accounts, proprieties and everything hidden. The worst thing is, some of these accounts and properties are in Olivia's name."

I feel the anger rising.

"What the actual fuck Keys?"

"Prez, I've checked the signature on the paperwork and it isn't Olivia's. I have every faith in her and I know for a fact she has no clue any of this is in her name."

"How do you know this?"

I trust Olivia, I know she wouldn't have known anything about the money or properties, otherwise she wouldn't have stayed so long at her dad's clubhouse. She definitely wouldn't have been wearing the scraps and hand me down clothes that she was.

"I told her I needed her signature on some paperwork so I could get her a bank card for the housekeeping account. She's been doing all the shopping recently. She read the whole of the agreement before she signed it to check I was telling the truth. Girls got street smarts and brains."

Pride swells in my chest.

Fuck, she really is the perfect girl and she is all mine.

"Okay, keep digging and get me a list of all properties, whose name they are in and all bank accounts too."

I turn to leave but stop in the doorway.

"Keys, do that after you've had a shower, food, and some sleep. You need to look after yourself so you can keep doing what you do best brother."

Nodding, he turns away from his computers and heads for the bathroom. Closing the door to his room, I head for my office. I want to call Judge to check in and let him know a little of what Keys found. He doesn't answer which is unusual. Every single time we have rung him, he has answered within a couple of rings. The uneasy feeling in my stomach is stronger, so I try him again with no luck. Yeah, something is definitely not right. Deciding to try Archer, seeing as his Prez isn't picking up.

"Archer."

Instantly his voice is off.

"Chaos, what's happened?"

"I was just about to ring you. It's not good and I hate that I am having to tell you this Chaos, but Judge is dead."

I say nothing for several minutes, just letting it sink in. Judge is dead. This is going devastate Liv.

"Dead?"

"Yeah, someone ran him off the road over the edge of a trail around here. His bike burst into flames, there was no saving him. Had to be identified by dental records. Fuck, it killed me seeing him like that."

I can only imagine how seeing not only a brother but your Prez like that will mess with your head.

"You getting support if you saw him like that Archer?"

This life is hard and, in my club, we don't mess around with our mental health. I know it is a taboo subject around a lot of men as we need to show we are strong and can handle anything. To me, it shows strength to admit you need help.

CHAOS

"Yeah, I'm good. We need to tell Liv before Dyno does."

"Why would Dyno be telling Liv?"

"Judge died two days ago, wanted to make sure it was him before we told you, but Dyno has been strutting around like he's won the lottery. Saying he's now Prez, even though we haven't voted on it and Judge hasn't had a funeral. Keeps saying how as club princess, Olivia's place is here."

I'm seething by this point.

Is he fucking for real?

"That bastard is not getting his hands on Liv. I've claimed her as my Ol' Lady. It's done. I wouldn't put it passed Dyno to be the one to run him off the road. I warned Judge to be careful."

"Chaos, we all warned Judge to be careful. Just keep Liv safe and we will keep you in the loop with funeral. I am sorry this has fallen on your shoulders to tell her. I wish it was different."

Fuck he sounds broken; I know him and Judge have been friends for a long time despite the age difference. It was almost as if Archer was a second son to Judge. Plus, Archer was close with Voodoo.

"I know, we both wish it was different, but I'll look after her and make sure she's okay. Keep me posted."

I just finished the call when Twisted bursts through the office door.

"Sorry Prez, but you need to come quick to the gate," he says out of breath and starts run back the way he came.

Fuck, now what? This day is going to hell.

Heading through the main room, I hear Liv screaming

97

outside and I take off at a run, heading for the gate. The sight that greets me makes my heart stop. Liv is on her knees, crying in pain, while screaming at someone at the gate. Riot has her pulled into him, trying to protect her and calm her down.

"What the fuck is going on?" I bellow, getting close to the gate.

I finally get a clear look at the person at the gate.

Jesus Christ.

Dyno is standing there, looking all proud of himself. Now I am closer, I can just make out what Liv is screaming.

"You fucking liar. Take it back."

The pain in her voice hits me straight in the chest.

"Liv, Sweetpea," I say, getting on the floor next to her and pulling her into my lap, cradling her in arms.

I stroke her hair and whisper to her that everything is going to be okay. My t-shirt is in her fist as she clings to me, sobbing.

"Make him take it back. My dad is not dead, he wouldn't leave me. Tell him Chaos, make him take it back," she begs me.

She is breaking my heart; I give Dyno the evil eye over the top of Liv's head.

"Olivia is our princess and belongs at home." Dyno says with a smirk on his face.

I really want to swipe that fucking smirk right off his face.

"She is my Ol' lady, already claimed her and voted on."

He drops the smirk and I fight to hide my smile. Now

is not the time to smile while Liv is still shaking in my arms.

"It has not been approved by our club," Dyno shouts angrily.

"Doesn't need to be, it was approved by her father who is the President. So, doesn't matter what the fuck you say."

"The President is dead and I am the new one. You don't have my permission and you never will."

I stand up with Olivia in my arms, I am not staying here with her to listen to this.

"You haven't been voted in as President, so don't get all excited yet."

I walk away and head straight for our room. Laying on the bed with Liv still in my arms, I hold her while she continues to sob.

"Please Declan. Please tell me he is the lying bastard I think he is."

"Oh, Sweetpea, I wish I could. I spoke with Archer just before the prospect came to get me. He told me it is true; I am so sorry Liv. He died in bike accident."

The scream of pain that rips from her body has been me holding her closer, while my ears are ringing, her scream was so loud. Within seconds, Riot, Dolla, Mayhem and Psycho all storm into my room.

"We heard her scream," Mayhem explains.

Nodding, I tell them it is true about Judge.

Riot crawls into the other side of the bed and curls himself around Liv.

"I am so fucking sorry petal. We are here if you need us."

"Thank you Riot," she says between breaths as she tries

to calm herself.

"We are all here for you Liv," Mayhem tells her.

"We got you," adds Psycho.

"You are family Liv; we will look after you," Dolla says.

"We will leave you in peace," Riot says as he unwinds himself from around my woman, and kissing her on the forehead.

I would be jealous if it was anyone else, but Liv has formed a close bond with all my brothers. Each of them takes it in turns giving her a hug and kiss on the forehead before leaving us in peace.

I hold her tightly in my arms while she cries herself to sleep.

FOURTEEN

OLIVIA

I'M depressed, I know I am but I just can't bring myself to care. I stay curled up in bed with Raze and King. They have hardly left my side for the past week. I hide my face in King's neck while I cry for what I have lost.

That is, it, I now have no family left.

Yes, I am well aware I have Chaos and the brothers but I mean blood family. My parents are now both gone and I have no clue where in the hell Voodoo is, but at this point he has been missing for so long, I fear he too has left me. Well, that is what my head is saying anyway, but my heart. My heart is saying a whole different thing. It still feels my dad and Voodoo as if they are alive. Not sure if that is just wishful thinking or our strong bond letting me know to keep fighting for them.

I haven't spoken to Declan about how I feel because I'm not sure if he will understand. Hell, I don't understand my feelings, so how am I expecting them to. I just don't fully trust what I am feeling. Declan has begged me to talk to some grief counsellor, he thinks might be able to help me. He's been amazing with me, so patient and kind. The first few days when I couldn't even function other than to go to the bathroom. he helped bathe, feed, and held me while I cried and generally talked me down off the ledge. At least now I can wash myself but I am still not eating. My stomach constantly feels sick and I cannot even think about food without wanting to be sick. I've lost weight and I can tell Declan is becoming really worried about me. I just can't bring myself to care. A knock at the door brings me out of my head. The door opens slowly and a handsome little face pops around it.

"Liv," Logan semi shouts in a hushed voice and dives for the bed. Raze just manages to move in time before Logan lands on him. He grumbles about moving but does it anyway, both dogs are so good with Logan, they never snap or snarl at him when he's maybe a little too rough with them.

"Hey Lo," I greet him as he snuggles himself into me.

Mayhem hoovers near the door.

"I'm sorry to do this to you Liv but I need to go into work for an hour or two and I have no one to watch Lo."

I hold Logan a little closer, his little body snuggling in and getting comfy in the bed with me.

"It's fine Mayhem. We will chill and watch films."

"Monsters Inc," comes muffled voice from under the covers with a little arm shooting out to do a fist bump. He loves his fist bumps.

"Yeah Lo, Monsters Inc," I chuckle for the first time since I learnt my dad died.

"You sure?" Mayhem asks but he is already edging out the door.

"Yes, I am sure. Just ask the prospect to bring him lunch up later."

"For both of you?"

"For Logan," I say getting sterner.

"Okay," he replies on a sigh, not really happy with my answer but do I give a fuck.

Once Mayhem has gone, we get all settled and I pop the film on Netflix. The dogs are snoring at our feet and Logan is curled up in my side with his head on chest. My arm tightens around him.

"Liv, why you so sad?" he asks in his little voice.

Fuck, fuck, fuck.

What do I say? He is only four years old; it's not my place to explain death to him. Who even as adults understand it?

"Sometimes adults are just sad."

Quick thinking, not.

"I don't like it when you're sad. It makes me sad."

Way to kick me while I'm down kid. Right in the feels too.

"Logan, I don't want you to be sad, but sometimes adults are going to be and that is okay but for me not to be sad, I need you to be my happy little chappy. Okay?"

He nods his head, gives me a blinding smile, and kisses me cheek. He melts my heart, he really does.

"You stealing my woman Lo man?"

Declan makes me jump as I didn't hear him come into the room.

"She is my Liv," he replies snuggling closer.

"I brought you a happy meal, its downstairs."

"MacDonald's," he screams, leaping from the bed at speed and running from the room.

"Good to know a MacDonald's comes before me," I grumble.

Declan chuckles and takes up the space Logan left.

"You will always come first with me, Sweetpea."

I curl closer to him and wrap myself around him.

"You have a good time with Lo?" he asks while stroking my hair. I love it when he does this, it instantly relaxes me.

"Kid is good company," I reply.

"Yeah, he really is. I wanted to talk to you about something. I know you said you didn't want to travel for your dads funeral. I heard and understand your reasons, I even agree with the whole Dyno is still a danger and whoever ran your dad off the road."

Okay, if he understands then why is he bringing it up again?

"I thought you might still like to do something, so I spoke with the brothers and we would like to have a memorial here for Judge. That way we can all pay our respects."

The tears fall and I am powerless to stop them. They really are the most amazing, thoughtful, and kind bunch of badass bikers I have ever met.

"Oh Sweetpea, we didn't mean to upset you. We

thought it would be something nice," he panics and the tears keep coming.

"You haven't upset me. I'm just so touched. Jesus why can't I get a grip of my emotions?"

Declan holds me tighter.

"Olivia, you have been through so much in such a short space of time. Of course, you are going to feel overwhelmed and your emotions are going to be running high but I promise you, things will get better."

He truly does always know just the right thing to say.

"Thank you, sometimes I feel like I am losing my mind," I admit

"How so?"

Do I tell him and be honest? If I can't be honest and tell him how I am truly feeling then what is the point of being in a relationship with him?

"I don't want you to think I'm crazy. My head fully understands that my dad has died and Voodoo probably has too, but my heart and my gut are saying something completely different. I don't know if it is just wishful thinking or if the connection, I have with them is so strong that I feel them. My heart and gut are telling me something is not right. They could still be alive. It's like I am at war with myself."

There I said it, out loud and yes, I sound crazy.

"Olivia, I need you to listen me. I don't think you are crazy. I've learnt over the years to trust my gut. It's never let me down and my gut tells me to trust your instincts. If your instincts are telling you something is not right then I will back you all the way, Sweetpea."

I'm shocked. I look into his eyes and all I see is sincerity. He really will back me up.

"Will you look into my dad's accident please? Just for my peace of mind?"

He holds me closer to him and kisses my head.

"I will get Keys to see what he can find, but don't be disappointed if he find nothing. I trust your gut Liv but I don't want you getting your hopes up."

Okay, I can sort of understand where he is coming from but if I'm to trust my gut then my dad is still alive.

"If you think I need to trust my gut then why shouldn't I get my hopes up?"

He sighs and moves me into his lap so I'm straddling him. He cups my face with his hands and looks directly into my eyes. I can see how serious he is.

"I trust your gut feeling Liv and I will back you. In backing you, I will also protect you as much as possible. Just because I believe you, doesn't mean it's the true either. Now, before you jump down my throat, I am not saying what you feel isn't the truth either. It would be naive and dangerous though not to consider all angles. So that being said, I will ask Keys to look into it for you. Depending on what he finds, we will see what our next move is."

Nodding in understanding, he kisses me.

FIFTEEN

CHAOS

HER lips are pressed against mine and she's hovering right over my crotch, which is growing tighter by the minute. Liv has been so depressed recently over her dads death, that sex has been the furthest thing from her mind. I understand that but fuck, I miss my woman.

I quickly pull my phone out and send a text to Keys to look into Judge's death more closely. I know she is grieving which can affect your emotions but her gut isn't the only one that's making itself known. Mine is screaming at me that something doesn't add up. No way Judge would have gone out like that, he was seasoned rider with years of experience. I throw my phone at the end of the bed all without breaking the kiss. Liv is now grinding down on me and practically getting herself off. My girl needs the release bad and I'm all for giving her what she needs.

"Declan," she moans.

My cock gets harder than I ever thought possible. Her

soft moans turning me on more. I slide my hands around her gripping her full ass and squeeze. Her moan gets a little louder and move from kissing her lips and slowly kiss down to her neck, nibbling a little as I go.

"Declan," she says begging.

"I know Sweetpea, just enjoy. I'll take care of you."

She nods and lifts her head giving me more access to her neck. I suck a little harder and feel her shiver. My girl likes that, *interesting*. I stop kissing her just long enough to pull her top over her head and remove her bra. Her tits are just a little more than handful and I have big hands. Liv throws her head back in pleasure as I suck on one nipple and play with the other. My fingers rolling her nipple between them and slight pinching them.

"I need... I need more."

I love it when she begs me.

Sliding her from my lap, I lay her on the bed and kiss down to towards her panties. Removing them, I widen her legs so I can see her glistering centre. My mouth waters at the sight of her wet pussy. Unable to stop myself, I dive in like starved man. I am a starved man, starved of my woman's pussy and she tastes amazing. I slip my tongue between her lips, licking from bottom to her clit, sucking when I get to the bundle of nerves.

"Declan," she screams as her orgasm ripples through her.

I slowly push my fingers into her channel, feeling her pulse around them, prolonging her pleasure. As she's coming down, I kiss back up until I reach her mouth. I plant a kiss on her soft plump lips as I line my cock up, slowly pushing inside her. She wraps her arms and legs around me, clinging onto me like her life depended on it.

"Hold on baby," I warn her before I start to piston in and out of her.

Her nails draw down my back spurring me on. I can't get enough of her; she feels like heaven. I start to feel the tingle at the base of my spine as she tightens around me. I can't hold off any longer and with shout, we come together. I roll onto my back as we fall back onto the bed, so I'm not crushing her. Her head is resting on my chest as I run my fingers through her hair, and we both catch our breaths as we just lie there, wrapped in each other, enjoying the quiet moment.

"Thank you," her voice is so soft and quiet I almost don't hear her.

"What are you thanking me for?"

"A little of everything."

Holding her a little closer to me, I kiss her head.

"You never have to thank me for having your back."

"It's more than that. The brothers and you have done so much for me in such a short space of time. You've all been so kind and welcomed me into your family. I have so many dreams and goals that I honestly never thought would be possible."

Jesus, she just gutted me. A small amount of kindness from the brothers has meant so much to her.

"I will do everything in my power to make every dream, wish and goal come true for you. I'm not the most expressive man, not good with words but I will show you every day just how you mean to me. I never thought I would ever have an Ol' Lady, it wasn't in the cards for me. Then you came along and from the first sight of you, I was gone. I couldn't get you out of my head. I had this urge to see you again, to be close to you. Not in weird a stalker creepy way."

This makes her giggle and smile. Her giggle the best sound I had ever heard, right next to the moans she makes when she comes. My new mission in life is to make her giggle and smile every day.

"Just know that I've fallen hard for you. Life won't be easier for us but I promise I will make it worth it."

She runs her hand down the side of my face, cupping my cheek.

"I think you're better with words than you think. Yes, a thousand times, yes to everything you just said. I don't need you to tell me how you feel every single day as then it would just become words and lose their meaning. Actions mean more than words and you show me every day with the little things you do. Little things that I don't think you realise you are doing."

She blows me away with just a few sentences. This woman amazes me every single day. Yes, she is struggling right now with her grief but she is dealing with it in a way that works for her. Each day I notice she's getting a little better and spending time with Logan has clearly helped her massively.

"Anything you want or need Sweetpea, I will gladly give you."

She gives me her blinding smile which has been missing recently.

"I'm hungry. Have the boys eaten yet?" she asks as she starts getting out of the bed and heading for the bathroom.

"No Liv, they haven't. Missed your cooking."

She smiles at me over her shoulder as she makes it to the bathroom door.

"I've missed cooking for them. Let me freshen up and I'll be down to whip something up for them."

With that, she heads into the bathroom and closes the door.

Yes, my girl is coming back!

SIXTEEN

OLIVIA

I'M starting to feel a little more like myself. I still miss Dad but I know he wouldn't want me to wallow in self-pity and depression.

Getting a quick shower and washing my hair, I feel more human. Eager to get back in the kitchen and out this bedroom, I dry and hurry to get dressed. I'm still trying to sort my shoe out as I hop out the room into the hallway, and run straight into what feels like a brick wall, bouncing off into the actual wall, then onto floor.

Really lady like and graceful Liv, for fuck sake.

Flicking my hair out of my face I look up at the giant brick wall that is Riot, who is currently leaning on the wall, clutching his stomach, while laughing his arse off.

Gentleman he is not.

"Erm, yeah no worries, Riot, I'm fine. Perfectly okay. Jackarse," I mumble, attempting to get off the floor again, not so gracefully.

"I'm soo.... sorry Liv baby but that was funny as shit. You looked like a human pinball."

He continues to laugh until Psycho appears from nowhere and smacks him across the back of the head.

"Fucker," he grunts and then helps me off the floor.

"Okay?" he checks while running his eyes over me to check that I am.

"Yeah, no thanks to that giant walking brick wall."

"Dumb as a brick wall," Psycho replies with a grin on his face.

We head down the hall with Riot behind us, still laughing. Getting into the main room, Chaos is sitting at the bar with Mayhem.

"What's funny?" Mayhem asks.

"Oh, you missed it. Liv came hopping out your room like an annoyed little bunny, bounced right into me and off again into the wall. So funny, she looked like a pinball," Riot states as he's still laughing.

Chaos does not look like he finds this funny.

"Fuck Sweetpea, are you okay? Did you hurt yourself?"

He's by my side in seconds, his hands running all over me, checking for himself that I am in face okay and not hurt. Mayhem is also now next to me, with his arm around my shoulders.

"Okay Liv?"

Jesus, it was only a little fall. I'm clumsy, so they need to get use to me falling off and into things. I have a wonderful skill of falling over fresh air.

"Yeah, I'm fine. You guys will have to get used to this. I'm seriously clumsy, but honestly it was kind of funny. Not graceful at all."

Mayhem gives my shoulders squeeze and smacks Riot across the back of the head.

"Why the fuck are people hitting me today?"

Bless him, he really is looking confused, rubbing the back of his head.

"You're an idiot. Your Presidents Ol' lady falls on the floor and you laugh."

You can see the wheels turning as he figures out maybe it's not as funny as he thinks.

"It was a, *'had to be there,'* moment, but she was okay."

Right, think I need to step in before Chaos gets his licks in.

"Honestly, Riot is right. It was kind of funny. I have my entertainment value. So, whose hungry?"

Tracker perks up from across the other side of the room in what can only be described as a Meerkat moment.

"Someone mention food?" he asks as he stands and makes his way over to us.

"You got bat hearing or something Tracker? You heard food from that far away?" I can't help but ask.

"If you're cooking then I would hear and smell it from miles away. What ya cooking me pretty lady?"

Laughing again, this is the most I have laughed since Dad passed.

"What you in the mood for? I'll see what we have, might need to do a shopping run though."

Chaos kisses my head as I turn to make my way into the kitchen, I stop and kiss his cheek. Smiling, I continue into the kitchen. Checking the fridge, freezer, and cupboards, I can see no one has thought to shop since I've mainly been in our room. The fridge is full of takeaway leftover boxes.

"Erm has no one cooked or shopped since I've been.... down?" I say not really sure how to put me being stuck in bed.

"Nicely put and no. I'm feeling seriously neglected," Dolla says joining me in the kitchen with Tracker.

"Poor baby," I say, patting his stomach

"Sweetpea, make a list of shit we need and I'll send a prospect or two to get it for you."

"Thanks love."

I get the shopping list pad and pen from the draw and start making a detailed list for the prospects. I even make sure I write the brands etc of what I want to ensure they don't get it wrong like last time they went without me.

Jesus, Mary, Joseph, and the wee donkey, that was one fuck up.

Once I've finished my list, I hand it over to Twisted and with a wink, he's gone.

I like Twisted, he has this natural ease to him and a bit of swagger. No way am I telling Chaos that, but then again, all the brothers have been amazing and I've formed friendships with all of them. Deciding to give the kitchen a good clean, I roll up my sleeves and get started.

It takes me a good hour to take all the out-of-date food out of the fridge, put it into the bin and clean it. All the surfaces are cleaned and I've even wiped the shelves in the cupboard down. All hot and sweaty, I decide to get some fresh air, so I slip out the backdoor unseen and slowly make my way around the front to sit on the picnic table, over near the shade of the trees. I just needing a moment to myself, I'm so close to the picnic table when I feel a hand over my mouth and around her around my waist. I start to panic; I can feel it rising and trying to pull me down. I try to take a deep breath to centre myself so I can figure a way out of this. I can't let them take me off the compound.

I'm being dragged over to a small hole in the fence, but we have to pass the bikes to get to it. Using all my might and strength, I raise my legs and start to kick. I swing my legs with everything I have and manage to unbalance my attacker enough that my foot collides with a bike, giving it enough momentum to rock and knock into the next one. My attacker freezes as we watch partly in horror as like a domino effect; each bike falls into the one next to it, with an almighty crash. Taking this as my moment, I bite the hand over my mouth causing him to yelp, moving his hand, he gives me enough room to scream.

"Chaos," I scream as loud as I possibly can.

The door to the clubhouse flies open and all the brothers pile out. Chaos is at the front with Psycho and Riot on either side of him and Mayhem behind them, with the rest of the brothers. Seeing everyone rushing outside seems to wake my attacker up and he's back to dragging me through the hole in the fence. I continue to scream as loud as I can and struggle as much as possible.

No fucking way am I making this easy on the fucker.

The minute he hears me, he takes off at a run with his gun out. I'm thrown in the van but I keep screaming his name as much as possible.

"Chaos," I scream with everything in me.

The door to the van closes, enveloping me inside as I continue to scream his name.

"Shut the fuck up bitch."

Before I can realise that I know the voice, I'm hit over the head and the darkness swallows me whole.

SEVENTEEN

CHAOS

CHILLING at the bar, Liv has been in the kitchen cleaning up a storm for nearly over an hour. Twisted is still out getting the shopping list she gave him, and knowing my girl, he will be a while longer too. Her list looked long and he's called twice already to check on a few things.

A huge crash sounds from outside and we all freeze for second before we all dash out the door to see what the fuck is going on. Her terror-filled screams will haunt me for the rest of my life as I watch my whole reason for being alive, taken from me. I want to fall to the ground as my knees feels weak under me but I can't. She needs me to keep my head and get her back.

"Prospects, get them bikes right and someone get hold of Twisted. Boys mount up in the cars," I shout heading for the them.

Mayhem is riding with me; Riot and Psycho are in one car and Tracker with Dolla in another. I notice in my rear-view mirror that Keys is running back inside, heading for his geek cave no doubt. Flooring it, I head out the compound and down the street that runs down the side of us, where the van has headed. I can make it out in the distance but they have a good head start on us. Upping my speed, I try to catch them up and Mayhem gets on his phone.

"Riot has taken the other side to see if he can cut him off. Keys is hacking traffic cams to trace them and is also bringing up Liv's tracker you put in her shoes."

Thank fuck, Keys and Tracker had the idea to hide GPS trackers on Liv. She has them in her shoes, one in a necklace I gave her and also a bracelet Logan made her.

I keep following the van but it's getting further away and I'm struggling to catch it up. Mayhem is beside me in the passenger seat on the phone with Keys, Riot and Dolla on a three-way call so everyone can keep in touch. The van turns a corner ahead and disappears, when we finally make it to the junction, it's gone.

"Fuck!" I yell, thumping my fist on the steering wheel.

No, this cannot be happening. I can't and will not lose her, when I have only just gotten her. If Dyno gets his hands on her, because let's be honest, we all know who has taken her, it will be nothing but pain for my girl. She doesn't deserve the life she would have with him. No woman deserves the life she would have with Dyno and his merry depraved band of men.

"Riot lost them too," Mayhem tells me with concern and anger written all over his face.

"We have to find her," I tell him in a pleading voice.

"Keys is trying to track for GPS chips but it seems they have a blocker or something. I don't know, he's geeking out and freaking out at the same time."

Jesus fuck, because that's reassuring.

I turn around and head back to the compound. Mayhem is still on his phone while I drive us back. I'm lost in my head thinking of all the things I could have done differently to keep her safe.

I failed her.
We failed her.

Myself and the brothers all promised she was safe. That we would protect her and yet, she is taken right from the middle of the compound. We need to take a closer look at our security so this never happens to her again. I know we haven't got her back yet but there is no way in hell I am not getting her back. I will burn this country, hell I will burn the world down hunting for her. Dyno hasn't met me properly yet but I am about to rain Chaos down on him. Parking the Car, I leap out and head straight to Keys geek cave.

"Prospect, get that hole in the fence fixed now," I yell as I pass them.

Heading down the hall, I don't even knock on his door, just storm in.

"Talk to me Keys," I demand.

I'm not in the mood for pleasantries or being fucking nice.

"He must be jamming the signal from the trackers as they are not showing. Last time they showed was when she was in the compound, so they were definitely working before she was taken. We know it was Dyno who took her, so I'm doing a deep dive into all the property he owns and checking the cameras around them to see if I can see the van, she was taken in."

I put my hand on his shoulder, I can see he is taking this really hard. Liv has come to mean a lot to all of us.

"Thanks brother, we will get her back. Let me know once you have something. I need to ring Archer and let him know what's happened."

Keys nods but never looks away from the screen. I head for my office and take a seat in my chair. I don't want to make this call but I know I have to and maybe Archer might have some information that can help. Taking a deep breath, I dial him.

"Chaos, how's Livie girl?" he asks

"Archer…" I start not knowing how really to start or finish.

"What's happened?" His voice instantly tight and not as relaxed as it was at the start.

"Dyno has taken Liv. I tried to catch them but we lost them in traffic. I'm sorry but I am going to get her back."

Silence is what greets me. Nothing but the heavy breathing of Archer trying to rain his temper in.

"Okay, we know its Dyno because seriously it will be no one else. Let me make some calls and put some feelers out. The boys and me will head your way, between us we will get her back."

I let go of the breath I didn't realise I was holding.

"Thank you, Archer."

"Anything for Livie girl. We've let her down too much in the past, we won't let her down again." With that he ends the call.

I stay in my office a little while longer just gathering my thoughts. I need to stay in control and level headed if I'm going to get Liv back safely. Knowing I have hidden myself away long enough and it will only take Archer around an hour and half to two hours tops to get here I leave my office. Its already been an hour since we spoke. Hitting the main room, I find it empty. Turning back around, I head to Keys room. Opening his door, I find the room cramped with all my brothers. Each and every one of them, including the prospects are helping him.

This is family.

"Archer and his boys are on their way. Should be here within the hour. Havoc, can you set rooms up please?"

Nodding, he places the laptop down and heads out. Mayhem who was manning one of the many computer screens, picks the laptop up and starts where Havoc left off.

"I think I found something," shouts Riot.

Keys whizzes past me on his office chair, nearly taking my toes with him if I hadn't managed to jump out of his way. His sole focus on the laptop he swiped out of Riot's hands. We all wait with baited breath to see what he's found. I feel my phone vibrating in my pocket, so I step out the room to answer.

"Chaos."

"Ahh Chaos, I think you may be missing something."

That fucking prick Dyno has called me to gloat.

CHAOS

Stepping back into the room, I tap Keys on the shoulder and point to my phone.

"Dyno you cocksucking leech. Yes, you do have something that doesn't belong to you, but don't worry, you won't have her for long"

His laugh bellows down the phone.

"You will never find her. Give it up, the best man won. I have the club and the princess. Nothing you or any of these biker wannabes can do anything about it."

I can, Keys is frantically clicking away at his computer, tracing the call. He makes a rolling motion with his fingers as if to say keep him talking.

"Yeah, how did a brainless idiot like you manage to take over a whole MC?"

I'm trying to goad him just enough so gives me more information than he means to, without pissing him off too much that he puts the phone down on me.

"That Chaos my friend, was the easy part. Judge was an old fool and his son an even bigger idiot. So easy to dispose of, like child's play really."

He's so cocky and arrogant; it is going to be his downfall.

Keys gives me a thumbs up to say he's got him.

"Well, you've got nothing to say now have you Chaos? Not so badass as you like to think. Say goodbye Chaos," he taunts and then second later, I hear the worst sound in the world.

"Chaos," Liv screams with pain and fear in her voice.

"Liv," I shout back.

With a last laugh, he ends the call.

Oh, he may think he's got the last laugh but I'll show

him a true man.

"He's about ten miles from here, in an old warehouse. I'll bring up the aerial maps and we can plan," Keys says as he's clicking away and his massive printer kicks into life.

"Print what we need. Church," I shout as I storm out and head that way.

"Twisted, send Archer and his men into church when they get here," Mayhem tells him from behind me.

"Chaos, Mayhem. I know prospects aren't allowed in church but Liv has grown to mean a lot to not only me but also all the prospects. Please, we want to help bring her home."

Mayhem and I share a look. We really do need to patch him in soon. Nodding, I head for church. We have a plan to make to get my girl back.

EIGHTEEN

OLIVIA

I feel cold. Not just a normal cold but a bone deep chill, that is causing the hair on the back of my neck to stick up and a fear like I've never felt before, to run through my entire body. I'm not a hundred percent sure where I am but deep down, I know where it's not. I keep my eyes closed and my breathing even, giving me time to wake properly. I listen for any noises but all I can hear is my own heart beating, which is good sign, and dripping water. Next, I take stock of body.

My head is killing me and my wrists feel sore as well as my shoulders. My shoulders hurt because it feels like I am hanging from them. A cold breeze runs across my skin, meaning I no longer have my clothes on.

That's not good.

I will not panic. I will not panic.

I keep chanting this in my head as I start to feel myself panic. The memories are starting to come back to me. I remember going outside to get some fresh air and cool down after cleaning the whole of the kitchen. A hand goes over my mouth, Rattle's voice appears in my ear, I remember kicking the bikes, screaming for Chaos. Chaos, he saw me, I know he did as he was running towards me. Then being thrown in the van and then darkness.

I should have known Dyno and his wanker crew had something to do with this. I take a deep breath and listening a little more to make sure I am alone; I slowly open my eyes. Taking a look around, I find that I'm hanging from the ceiling in a small concrete room. You can smell the damp and musk in the air. A door is in front of me and a chair sits in the corner. A old, gross stained mattress, sits on the floor in the other corner and that is all.

Looking down, I can see that I'm at least still wearing my underwear but the rest of my clothes and shoes have gone. So even if I tried to escape, I would be doing it in only a bra and panties.

Perfect, makes it harder to escape then doesn't it.

Looking up, the chains around my wrists are connected to a hook in the ceiling, that is attached to a control unit on the wall. This is not just the work of Dyno. No way that thick, stupid son of bitch had put this much planning into anything. The door suddenly opens and Lizard enters.

"Ah you're finally awake princess," he sneers at me.

I choose to ignore him as Dyno and Rattle come in behind him.

"Her being awake makes it more fun," Rattle says as he runs his hand up my side and grabs my right breast roughly.

Knowing full well it will leave a bruise.

I try my best not to react but it's painful.

"Don't be brave Liv. We will make you scream," Rattle taunts me.

Dyno appears and hits Rattle in the face.

"Hands off until I'm done with her. She's mine," he demands, like he's still in charge.

Rattle gives him an evil look.

Oh, there seems to be some discord amongst them. I might be able to use that to my advantage.

"Be good boy now and do as your told," I say as sarcastic as possible.

"No one tells me what to do," Rattle growls.

"I'm your president and you will do as I say," Dyno demands, with his holier-than-thou tone.

"No one said you would be President," Lizard finally joins in.

The three of them then start to argue between themselves while I just hang here watching them, like monkeys in a zoo.

"Shut the fuck up, letting a gash get you like that. Fucking idiots," Guts says, finally showing face as he drags my brother Voodoo into the room, throwing him on floor at my feet in a bloodied heap.

I have to blink several times to make sure I really am seeing my brother. He's been missing for so long; I was starting to believe he really was dead and had left me.

"Voodoo," I scream.

I'm watching him carefully, holding my breath until I see his chest rise and fall.

Thank god, he's still alive.

"Tie him to the chair. This might make her co-operate with us," Guts says as Rattle pulls Voodoo up and quickly ties him to the chair in the corner.

"Now girl, I want all the details on the Road Wreckers businesses," Guts demands.

He's is off his rocker.

"Go to hell, I ain't tell you shit," I spit back at him.

He is a lot quicker on his feet than I thought, as his fist drives into my stomach, causing me to cry out.

"You will talk, just depends if it's the hard way or the easy one. Doesn't matter to me."

The smirk on his face tells me there is no easy way and Guts is the one in charge.

"I can't tell you something I don't know. The women aren't told any club business." I say, which is true.

"I think you know more than you are letting on."

I feel his hand hit my cheek as he backhands me, followed by another punch to my stomach. I hear something crack.

Fuck, there goes a rib.

He hits me a few more times and I'm now struggling to take in a full breath as my chest hurts from his punches. His rings that adorn his hands have cut into me and I can feel the blood slowly trickling down my skin. I hang my head, unable to hold it up any longer from being used as Guts personal punching bag.

"Enough," I manage to say on a wheeze.

"Let me tell you a little story about your daddy. How he

stole not only my club but also my woman. You see, I should have been the next President, not Judge. He was always weak. Just like your mum, she was mine first before Judge got to her, but you killed her. You took her away from me."

Guts has lost it now and is screaming at me. I had no clue he and my mum ever had any sort of relationship before my dad. No one has mentioned it, but then why would they? She was gone. Dad loved my mum and from the pictures I have seen of them together, she loved him too.

"You look just like her. He even named you after her too. My Olivia was the sweetest girl. You really do look so much like her," he says as his hand is stroking my face.

I try to move my face away from his touch, but he grips my chin between his fingers.

"Leave her alone," comes a groan from the corner.

"Voodoo," I whisper quietly.

Guts lets go of my chin and I turn my head to see Voodoo shooting daggers at him.

Thank God, he's sort of okay.

"Voodoo," I whisper again.

He smiles, well as much as his poor battered and bruised face can, and gives me a cheeky wink. There's the brother I have missed so much. His face then changes from my loving older brother to Voodoo, badass biker.

"It's not like you're in a position to give anyone orders, is it?" Guts laughs.

"Mum never loved you, she always loved Dad. You would've made the worst President in history. The club would have been destroyed in months with you running things. You're no man, a real man doesn't go after those weaker than him. You are fucking pathetic," Voodoo tells him.

I know what he is trying to do but I wish he wouldn't. He wants the attention on him, so Guts will leave me alone. Guts stalks towards Voodoo and starts punching him. He can't even defend himself. I turn my head away and notice Rattle has moved closer, so he's now right next to me.

"Your brother thinks he's protecting you, but he's only distracted Guts, giving me the chance to have my way," he whispers in my ear.

His hand slides inside my panties, touching where he has no business touching me. I move my hips trying to get away from him, but the second his fingers touch my skin; I dig deep and find a new strength I need to get out of this alive. I have to keep faith that Chaos and the brothers will find me.

"Get your hands off me," I bite back.

He grins as his fingers slide inside me, I bite the inside of my cheek to stop from crying out, the metallic taste of blood filling my mouth.

"Don't hold back on my account princess. You scream so pretty."

With that, he bites my nipple and I can't hold scream in any longer and I'm thrashing to get his fingers from inside of me.

"What did I tell you," Guts shouts, diving for Rattle as the pair of them fall to floor in heap.

CHAOS

As they roll around the floor, Dyno and Lizard are still arguing over who is President, completely ignoring everything else happening around them, too busy locked in their heated argument. Unable to help myself, I chuckle.

They look like a comedy sketch gone wrong, for fuck's sake.

Feeling a hand on me, I swivel round to see Voodoo has gotten loose and is lifting me down.

"Let's get out of here sis."

Falling into his arms, we hobble through the door, closing it behind us. They even left the keys in the lock; we quickly lock the door as the banging starts. Removing the keys from the lock, we slowly make our way down the concrete hall. Leaning on each other for support, as I cradle my left arm across my ribs, trying to offer my chest some relief. I'm also pretty sure my left shoulder is dislocated as that arm is floppy. We pass a few doors but suddenly I stop.

"What is it sis? We need to get out of here," Voodoo asks.

Slowly, I turn and make my way to the door we just passed, placing my hand it.

"We need to open it," I tell him.

Voodoo looks me in the face for a few minutes, he must see something in my eyes because he nods and starts trying the keys to find the right one. Once the door finally swings open, I gasp and fall to the floor.

NINETEEN

CHAOS

ARCHER and his boys have arrived. We're all cramped in church, going over the plans of the old warehouse and surrounding area that are spread over the table. Riot and Psycho have their heads together, planning with help from Archer. The rest are checking what arsenal we have available between us. Guns are really not readily available in the UK but we have a few on hand, just in case. Plus, a few smoke bombs etc, just in case they are ever needed and right now, I'm glad we do.

"Right, we have a plan. Dyno is so cocky; he's not going to think we can find him. Especially as he seems to be blocking GPS signals, so we have the element of surprise. We take the cars and go in as one. Just drive straight up and attack. No sneaking up on them or anything. That is what they will be prepared for," Riot says.

"So, we are aiming for the surprise bull in a china shop approach?" Archer chuckles.

"Yeah essentially. A wham, bam, thank you cocksucker," Riot replies with a smirk.

I roll my eyes at Riot's description; he really does have a way with words.

"Okay, sounds like a plan. Let's mount up and go get my girl," I nod and we all make our way out of church and to the club cars we have.

I'm in the passenger seat with Psycho driving. Mayhem and Riot are in the car behind, everyone else is divided between the remaining two cars and van. Ten miles is not that far but sitting here, it feels like it takes us hours to get just outside the warehouse. I just want my girl back. He best not of have hurt her. We all pile out the cars and van and I stop to take a look around. It's quiet. Too quiet. Psycho is also looking at me with the same thought. There are no bikes or cars parked out front, other than our own. Riot comes jogging from around the corner.

"There are four bikes and one van parked around the back. There's no sounds coming from inside and also no one about that I can see," he tells us.

"Be ready and tread carefully," I warn.

"Archer, Foggy and Mayhem, follow me around the back," Riot says as they all move to the back of the building.

The rest of us slowly make our way inside the building, it is eerily quiet. We come across an abandoned reception area, checking empty offices and bathrooms as we go. There's nothing but dust, debris, and a few rats. Finally, we make it to what must be the main manufacturing floor. You make out the chains and old bits of machinery still laying around undisturbed. We meet up with the rest of the brothers in the middle of the room.

"Nothing," Riot confirms.

"She has to be here. They have to be here," Mayhem shouts.

He really has gotten close with Liv. I stand a little away from the rest of the group, just looking around. I can feel her, yes that sounds girly and pathetic but fuck it. Liv is the missing part of my soul, so I know when my other piece is close.

"She's here," I say.

"How do you know?" Archer asks.

A smirk appears on Trader's face. He knows, him and his Ol' lady have been together since they were teenagers.

"Anyone check the basement?" Twisted calls from the far side of the room.

I knew that fucker would make the perfect brother.

"Need to patch that fucker quick," Psycho mutters next to me.

Nodding, I make my way over to Twisted, where he is opening a large metal door. We follow a short corridor before coming to a set of concrete stairs going down. The thudding of our boots echo in the stairwell, as we thunder down them to find another corridor of rooms. Slowly making our way down, we pass closed doors, taking time to check the handles, all of them are locked. We pass an open doorway and taking a second to look in the room, its empty. I start to move away, when I catch movement out the corner of my eye. Moving further into the room, I notice an open bathroom door, there standing in the doorway is Olivia. A very beaten Olivia, cradling her arm.

"Liv," I breath.

"Declan?" she whispers as more of a question as if she's not believing her eyes.

Within seconds, she is in my arms and all is right with my world. I hold her a little tighter and a soft painfilled groan reaches my ears.

Fuck, she's hurt and I'm squeezing the life out of her.

As I step away, Riot appears next to me with no shirt on and quickly pulls it over Liv's head.

Jesus, I was so happy and relieved to see her, I didn't notice she was only in her underwear.

My heart stops in my chest and panic starts to fill me.

Please god no. Please tell me we are not too late.

"You're not too late," she says as she wraps her good arm around my waist and buries her face in my chest.

My arms automatically come around her and my heart starts beating again.

"Thank you, brother," I choke as the emotion of having my girl back in my arms starts to get to me. Riot just pats me on the back as he steps away. I lift Liv into my arms and start to carry her out the room.

"Wait," she suddenly calls, lifting her head.

We all freeze and it's then I then notice two more people have joined our group. The Tribal Bones brothers have completely shocked looks on their faces. I realise that the two people are Voodoo and Judge. Liv was right, neither of them are dead. Both look like they've been to hell and back though. Liv reaches out to Psycho and hands him some keys.

"Last room on the right. They are all locked in there," she tells him.

Shock covers most of our faces at that admission.

"What all of them?" Psycho asks.

Liv nods her head and then lays back on my shoulder.

"Get me out of here, please," she tells me.

She doesn't need to be asked twice. Giving Psycho a chin lift, he knows what to do. I turn and make my way out of the basement and Mayhem is in front of me opening doors. A quick check behind me and I notice Foogy is helping Voodoo with Trader helping Judge. Ford and Archer have stayed behind to help Psycho. Everyone else is leaving with us. Leaving the van here, I slide into the back seat of the car and Mayhem jumps into the driver's seat.

"We need to get to the hospital," I tell him.

Nodding, he sets off. I hold Liv a little tighter and kiss her hair. She is covered in bruises; her hair is matted with dried blood; her face is also starting to swell a little. It feels like she's struggling to breath. and I start to panic.

"Liv, you, okay?"

She slowly opens her eyes and I panic more as I can see the fear in her eyes. She opens her mouth to speak but no words come out.

'Liv, stay with me baby, I need you to stay with me. Mayhem drive faster," I shout.

He can hear the panic in my voice and the car picks up speed. The warehouse is close to the hospital, so it's not far to go.

"Liv please, don't leave me. I love you," I beg.

CHAOS

Mayhem flies into the hospital and stops right outside the emergency doors. The passenger door swings open and Twisted is there helping me out with Liv still in my arms. Mayhem must have run inside. We run into the hospital to be greeted with Mayhem shouting for help. A nurse ushers me through and tells me to lay Liv down on a bed. A doctor appears and I'm pushed out of the cubical.

"Go wait in the waiting room and we will come find you. What's her name?" The nurse asks.

I just stand there, watching the doctor and another nurse start to assess Liv.

"Olivia Banks," Mayhem replies for me.

"Okay, go wait in reception," she orders as she turns back around and closes the curtain, so I can no longer see Liv.

"Come on brother, let's go wait," Mayhem says and steers me back the way we came.

I take a seat in the ugly, uncomfortable plastic chairs, resting my elbows on my knees, and dropping my head into my hands.

"I can't lose her," I choke on the words, as my fear spills from my mouth.

"You won't. That girl is fighter and she loves you. No way is she giving you up without fighting like hell. She could have given up at any point while she was taken, but she didn't and she won't now."

He sounds so sure that I have to believe him. Mayhem is my best friend and he wouldn't lie to me. Not about something as important as this.

IT feels like hours have passed and still no update. Slowly all the brothers have been joining us. In the end, there is that many of us, we are now waiting in a private room. I think my pacing and growling at staff was scaring them.

Do I care? Not a single fucking bit. I need to know something, anything.

Voodoo and Judge have also joined us after getting patched up. Both are okay really, just a little battered and dehydrated but neither would be admitted. Finally, after what feels like half of my life but looking at the clock, it's only been five hours, a doctor comes into the room.

"Olivia Banks' family?" he asks.

"I'm her man, this is her dad and her brothers," I tell him, standing up.

He nods, and thank God he doesn't ask any further questions.

"Olivia is going to be fine. During her attack, a rib fractured at some point, a small piece of bone dislodged and punctured her lung, causing it to collapse. We took her into surgery and repaired the puncture, re-inflating her lung. Her left shoulder was dislocated and this has also been set back into place. She has a lot of bruising, swelling and cuts. She needs rest and to heal, but otherwise, she will make a full recovery."

I feel like I can finally breath but a ton of guilt lands

directly onto me, causing me to drop into my chair.

Did I cause this? When I squeezed her too tightly?

"Chaos, what's wrong? I thought you would be happy?" Judge asks. The doctor is standing there looking at me.

"Did I cause her lung puncture when.... when I hugged her? Did I squeeze too tight?"

I had to ask and I can barely get the question out.

"No son, you didn't. The bone would have chipped on impact and then her moving around would have caused it to make a bigger impact. You did nothing wrong," the doctor reassures me.

I think he's lying but he's the expert.

"I need to see her. When can I see her," I demand.

"I will take you to her now," the doctor tells.

I get up and follow him out the room and down the hospital corridors until we reach the ICU unit, and the doctor turns to face us all.

"One at time, for only a few minutes and then someone can stay overnight with her," he warns.

Nodding, I go first. There laid on white sheets, looking so small and vulnerable, lays my heart. Machines beep all around us. I slowly lower into the chair at the side of her bed and take her hand in mine, pouring my heart out.

"You gave me such a scare Sweetpea. I thought you were leaving me. I love you so much and I cannot live in this world without you. We have an amazing future ahead of us. So many plans. I will build you the house of your dreams right on the compound, so you are always safe. We can have as many children as you like or none at all. You will want for nothing and feel loved, cared for and safe for the rest of your life. A very long happy life."

Tears are falling down my cheeks onto her hand, as I press kisses to her palm over and over.

"I love you too. yes, to all of that and more," a croak startles me.

"Jesus fuck Liv, I love you," I tell her as I stand, leaning over, kissing her head.

"Love you too Declan," she says with a smile on her face.

Life is now exactly as it should be.
Olivia and me, Ride or die.

TWENTY

OLIVIA

I can go home, finally. I've been stuck in this awful hospital room for just over a week. Declan has struggled to leave my side. After the first few days, I had to force him with the help of Mayhem to go home and shower properly, eat and get some sleep in a proper bed. He's been sleeping on a pull out in my hospital room, which can't be comfy at all. Plus, he needs some proper food in him. Hospital food is disgusting, how can they expect people to get better, if this they are feeding them this crap.

Today though, I get to go home and sleep in my own bed. Well Declan's bed but still. I've had a few nightmares and I can see Declan watching me as if I'm going to break. He hasn't come right out and asked me what happened in that basement. I'm glad because I don't want to tell him. I know in the back of my mind, he won't see me any different but knowing another man had touched me like that, I worry he would treat my differently. I'm not worried about getting intimate with Declan, I don't flinch or anything now when he touches me. My nightmares are not about what Rattle did to me. They are about Voodoo and Dad. I unlock the door and Dad is dead on the other side. Voodoo dies tied to that chair.

I know Psycho and Riot took care of the Wanker crew. They can't hurt me anymore and I think that is why I am able to slowly move passed what has happened. It will take time and I'm not over it just yet. I will never forget it but I will be able to move forward. That is due to love and support from Declan and the brothers. Each of them has visited me every day, bringing flowers, chocolates, things to read, a little present, just something to show they are thinking of me and care. For big badass bikers, they really are just soft teddy bears at heart.

For the next part of my recovery and getting on with my life is not something I am looking forward to talk to dad about. He has mentioned a few times about when I come home things will be different at the club, but the thing is, I am home. Home is with Declan and the rest of the Road Wreckers. Logan has become a huge part of my life and has drawn me get well soon cards and pictures. He truly is the sweetest little boy. Mayhem has even brought him to visit once I moved from the ICU to a normal ward. He was so careful giving me a hug.

One day, I hope I have a boy of my own, just as sweet as Logan is, but that is in a few years' time. I want to enjoy life with Declan first and find the person I am now that I'm free from the Wanker crew. I honestly hope dad understands. I spoke to Voodoo yesterday when he visited and he understood. He told me to be honest with dad and he would be sad to not see me every day but he only wants what is best for me and what makes me happy. The Road Wreckers make me happy; Declan makes me happy. For once I am excited about the future and all the possibilities it holds for me.

"Ready to break out of this joint Sweetpea?" Declan asks as he enters my hospital room.

"I was born ready," I reply in my best Sally Fields from Smokey & The Bandit impression.

It's my favourite film and Declan's too.

He chuckles and grabs my bag from the bed.

"Let's go start the rest of our lives Sweetpea."

"I can't wait," I smile back at him.

THE END

DEDICATION

Oh My God. It feels so good to type, 'The End,' for Olivia and Declan's story. It was not the story I thought it would be. It has been the hardest one I have ever written and has taken me a lot longer than I thought it would. Chaos is a man on his own and does things his way. His way is to stop talking to me for long periods of time and changing his mind a million and one times too.
But we got there in the end.

I hope you love them both as much as I do and also the rest of the brothers. Each is getting their own books and this is not the last you have heard from Tribal Bones either. Voodoo and Judge are as much a force of nature as Chaos and the Road Wreckers.

It has been a privilege, honour, and a joy to work with Ruby, Amy, and Ellie on this series. All three ladies are my absolute idols, so to work with them and learn from them has been joy.
Thank you for making this so much fun. You all rock.

A huge thank you to my girls Kate, Helen, and Tracy. You have forced to me to keep going when I wanted to give up. You have cheered me on and giving me the kick up the butt when I needed it.

Maria Lazarou, beautiful Maria, my editor, and friend. Who

has the patience of a saint. Thank you for sticking with my unorganised ass. I promise I will try to be better in future... we both know I'm always going to be last minute.

To Lee at Coffin Designs, my cover kicks ass. You rock my friend. You brought Chaos to life.

To my long-suffering husband, thank you for being the amazing man you are. For understanding when I needed to be an absent wife, hiding out in the lovely writing cave you made for me. Bringing me cups of tea, and rubbing my shoulders from being hunched over a laptop for so long. You are my biggest champion and support; I love you ever more for it. You can have your wife back now.... well until the next book.

The biggest thank you goes to you, my readers. Thank you for reading my books, leaving amazing reviews. Yes, I read every single one. I write for you.
I hope you enjoy Chaos, Olivia, and the rest of the motley crew.

Until next time....

Love Claire
xxx

SERIES ORDER

CHAOS
President
Claire Shaw

MAYHEM
V- President
Ruby Carter

PSYCHO
Enforcer
Ellie R Hunter

RIOT
Sergeant At Arms
Amy Davies

OTHER BOOKS BY CLAIRE

SONS OF HAVOC MC- TEXAS CHAPTER

Prez – Prequel

Joker

Carrie's Strength

Tank

Havoc Christmas

Wire- Coming Soon

SONS OF HAVOC- PHOENIX CHAPTER

Bishop- Coming Soon

CLAIRE SHAW

ABOUT THE AUTHOR

USA Today Best-Selling Author Claire is a Yorkshire lass born and bred. She lives there with her husband, two fur babies, and a large crazy extended family. Claire is also a huge country music fan and has a bit of an eclectic taste.

Claire has been involved with the indie community for many years now, attending signings but also as a PA for authors. Those authors encouraged Claire to put her ideas and life experiences on paper.

Believing reading is an escape from the pressures of real life, Claire is an avid reader and loves the joy it brings to people.

SOCIAL LINKS

Facebook
https://www.facebook.com/Claire-Shaw-Author-113232580058299/

Facebook Group
https://www.facebook.com/groups/662963237528957/

Instagram
https://www.instagram.com/claireshawauthor/

Goodreads
https://www.goodreads.com/author/show/17201274.Claire_Shaw

Printed in Great Britain
by Amazon